A dead silence came
over the cavern,
and all heads turned to look
up at Regdar. Mouths fell open,
and there was a wave of gasps.

Regdar smiled and looked
across the bizarre scene.
On the other side of the pit sat
a burly humanoid, much bigger
than the goblins around him.
It stood slowly and sneered
at Regdar.

Hobgoblin, Regdar thought.
I hate hobgoblins.

From the creators of the greatest roleplaying game ever come tales of heroes fighting monsters with magic!

By T.H. Lain

The Savage Caves

The Living Dead
(August 2002)

Oath of Nerull
(September 2002)

City of Fire
(November 2002)

The Bloody Eye
(January 2003)

Treachery's Wake
(March 2003)

THE SAVAGE CAVES

T.H. Lain

THE SAVAGE CAVES

Cover art by Todd Lockwood
First Printing: July 2002
Library of Congress Catalog Card Number: 2001097130

9 8 7 6 5 4 3 2 1

US ISBN: 0-7869-2845-X
620-88220-001-EN

U.S., CANADA,
ASIA, PACIFIC, & LATIN AMERICA
Wizards of the Coast, Inc.
P.O. Box 707
Renton, WA 98057-0707
+1-800-324-6496

EUROPEAN HEADQUARTERS
Wizards of the Coast, Belgium
P.B. 2031
2600 Berchem
Belgium
+32-70-23-32-77

Visit our web site at **www.wizards.com**

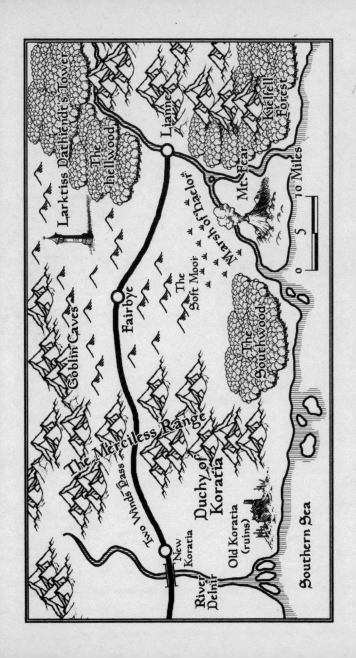

Prologue… The huge enchanted mace smashed into the side of the little goblin's head hard enough to send teeth riding a spray of blood through the quivering shreds of its ruined cheek. The goblin's name was Rvnj, and he fell to the cave floor in a wet heap.

Tzrg held his breath, eyes glued to the enormous hobgoblin who had just killed Rvnj for sneezing. The enormous hobgoblin had an equally enormous name: Rezrex. It was a name that was hard for goblins to say, just like it was hard for goblins to resist him.

Rezrex opened his wide mouth and laughed silently. His chest rose and fell in shuddering spasms. Tzrg and the other goblins could only watch in stunned, terrified silence. This went on for a long time, and all the while Tzrg forced himself not to make eye contact with any of his fellow goblins. He knew they were looking at him, waiting for him to do something, hoping he would put an end to this mission, which they all knew was a bad idea. Some of them were maybe even hoping he would do something about Rezrex—kill him or something. Of course, such a thing was impossible.

Rezrex was in charge because Rezrex decided to be in charge, and if anyone had anything to say about it, they would join Rvnj in a bleeding heap on a cave ledge, just like Rvnj joined Fkfk, Mrwk, and Nfjt who had been killed by Rezrex in the few days after the hobgoblin had first arrived in the caves of the Stonedeep Tribe.

When Rezrex stopped laughing he narrowed his bulging eyes and sneered, holding one long, thick finger in front of his lips and hefting the mace. The weapon was the most beautiful thing Tzrg had ever seen, and he had trouble keeping his eyes off it. It was made of half a dozen different shiny metals Tzrg didn't recognize. It didn't glow or burst into flames or conjure ghosts or anything, but it looked like it must be magical, so all the goblins just assumed it was. Rezrex seemed fine with that assumption.

Tzrg joined the other goblins in nodding their understanding and promise to Rezrex—they'd be quieter for the rest of the mission. Rezrex must have believed them, since he didn't kill anyone else, just waved them up into the dark shaft that twisted farther and farther away from Stonedeep territory. The shaft was taking them straight up to the home of the Cavemouth Tribe.

The goblins, strung together on ropes made from hive spider silk, had followed Rezrex a long, long way up the shaft. The hobgoblin came to a stop well over eighteen feet below the Border Sink, which marked a sort of no-goblin's-land between the Stonedeep and Cavemouth tribes. Rezrex turned and caught Tzrg's eye. He waved and pointed up, then flashed three fingers. Tzrg knew that if he pretended he didn't understand, which was his first impulse, Rezrex would kill him and try one of the other goblins. He made himself not sigh and stepped quietly up toward the hobgoblin, grabbing two goblins he knew to be good dark-fighters as he passed them. They approached Rezrex, and the hobgoblin swung aside, waving them on into the darkness ahead.

As they passed, Tzrg couldn't help but be amazed at the size of the hobgoblin. Rezrex was impressive, indeed. Twice as tall as the tallest goblin Tzrg had ever seen, Rezrex outweighed any goblin by more like three times. His arms—all muscle crisscrossed with bulging veins under his rough, hairy skin—were as big around as Tzrg's waist. His skin was darker than Tzrg's, who was the same dull orange as the rest of his tribe. Rezrex looked more red than yellow, with dark reddish-brown fur along his forearms, chest, and jaw line. His face wasn't quite as flat as Tzrg's, his nose thinner and more defined, his ears still pointed but smaller. Tzrg had heard that hobgoblins looked like a cross between a goblin and a human, but since Tzrg had never seen a human, he couldn't be sure if that was true or not.

Rezrex's clothes weren't too much better than Tzrg's, mostly animal hides and leathers mixed with stolen or found items. Rezrex wore pieces of what must have been armor. The idea of that fascinated Tzrg. The hobgoblin could be hit and not get wounded.

But it was the hobgoblin's eyes that Tzrg found most unsettling. They were smaller than any goblin's but shone with an evil intelligence that scared Tzrg as much as the mace did.

Rezrex scowled at Tzrg, who realized he'd been staring at the hobgoblin. Tzrg hurried off before his face was smashed in. The two goblins he'd brought with him, Nlnz and Frsj, were smart enough not to look at Rezrex. They just moved past him as quickly and as quietly as possible.

Tzrg knew why Rezrex had sent them forward. The hobgoblin must have heard something. Ahead of them the shaft narrowed to maybe seven feet in diameter and slanted at an angle that made climbing a whole lot easier. Considering that the Border Sink—a small crystal pool on a sharp-sided ledge fed by a cold waterfall from the surface—was just above them, it was surprisingly dry. The uneven floor turned up on each side to form natural shelves that ran along the length of the tunnel at about a goblin's height. The walls were smooth, layered with flowstone that made them slippery in spots. There were no sharp edges.

The shadows atop the shelves were deep—a good place to hide and set up an ambush. Tzrg, having never been this far from Stonedeep caves, didn't know if there were side passages leading out from the tops of the shelves. If there were, it would really be a perfect ambush point—you could throw a couple of javelins, and if things didn't go your way, you could get the hell out of there.

Tzrg tightened his grip on his javelin and pressed on, his ears twitching forward so he could hear better, his nose drawing in whatever stray scents might help, his eyes wide to see as deep into the shadows as he could. The three of them knew how to climb without making too much noise. Water was dripping somewhere

3

far above, and a nice juicy cave beetle scuttled along its way above his head. Tzrg resisted the temptation to eat it. The crunch of the bug's shell in his mouth might give them away.

Tzrg felt a hand on his arm and turned to see Frsj, who pointed to the shelf on the right side of the tunnel and nodded three times. Frsj had good eyes and an even better nose. Tzrg looked in the direction Frsj had pointed.

There was a sound like a female whispering, and Tzrg felt a breeze brush past his right arm. Another sound, a dull thump, followed quickly, and Tzrg turned to see a javelin protruding from Frsj's chest. Frsj was looking down at it with a confused expression. He didn't seem to be in any pain. He just hung from the rope he had tied around his waist at one end, and to Tzrg and Nlnz at the other.

Tzrg screamed two words: "*Bwlnk gbn!*"—an order to attack—and ran deeper into the tunnel as two more javelins swished past to clatter down the shaft behind him.

Nlnz followed close, almost tripping Tzrg just as they both saw the goblins hiding on the shelf. There were three of them, pressed into the shallow space on the side of the tunnel. They were hefting javelins, and without bothering to take the time to aim, Tzrg tossed his own javelin at the middle ambusher.

Tzrg's javelin went wide of its mark but sank into the shoulder of the goblin next to Tzrg's target. The enemy goblin squealed in pain and reached up to curl his fingers around the shaft of the javelin still sticking out of his shoulder. Nlnz's javelin clattered off the cave wall behind the middle goblin, who seemed confused and offended at being the obvious target of choice. It was nothing personal, of course, it was just that if you aim for the middle of three and miss, you might hit one of the other two. It was an old goblin tactic that had succeeded for Tzrg this time.

The first goblin in line lifted another javelin, and Tzrg jumped at him. It wasn't something Tzrg was normally apt to do, but these were desperate times. Compared to the folly of the whole mission, jumping at an armed opponent who had the twin advantages of the high ground and familiar territory wasn't so foolish.

Tzrg wished he'd remembered to pull his dagger before he landed on the middle goblin. Instead, they started wrestling. Tzrg was lucky at least to the extent that the middle goblin didn't know how to wrestle either. They were all elbows and grunting. The added weight of Frsj on the end of his rope didn't help Tzrg.

The goblin on the right pulled the javelin out of his shoulder with a wet *pop!* and a high-pitched wail. Nlnz followed Tzrg's lead and jumped up onto the shelf as well. With javelin in hand, Nlnz managed to slip off the side of his opponent's guard, avoiding the ambusher's stab at him with the sharp javelin. Nlnz sank his own sharpened stick into the ambusher's throat. There was a gurgling sound, and the goblin died just as Tzrg managed to get his dagger free.

Tzrg pushed back against his opponent's face in order to get his arm in between them and stab the middle goblin. That saved Tzrg's life—the wounded ambusher jabbed between Tzrg and the middle goblin, obviously aiming at Tzrg. Instead, the already bloody javelin that once belonged to Tzrg found its mark in the side of Nlnz's face. It dug a deep, nasty, ragged furrow in Nlnz's dull yellow skin, and blood burst out of the wound. Nlnz made a deep, sick sound as he died.

Tzrg sliced through the spidersilk rope that joined him to his two dead friends, then he reached out and grabbed the javelin with his left hand and stabbed the middle goblin in the ribs with the dagger he held in his right. The dagger was a little rusty and not as sharp as it once was, but it was a fine weapon, made by elves and stolen by Tzrg's great-grandfather before Tzrg was born. It was the knife of the chief of the Stonedeep Tribe and had been carried by

Tzrg's ancestors for generations, until Rezrex came and made himself chief.

The middle goblin didn't die at first, but he stopped fighting. Tzrg took that time to slash out to his side, cutting the wounded goblin's throat so that a waterfall of blood washed over the shelf. The dead goblin released his grip on the javelin, and Nlnz's limp body fell away in the other direction.

Tzrg, still holding the javelin, slid backward off the shelf and called, "*Mjk nlvdv!*" to warn Rezrex and the other goblins of the falling bodies.

The middle goblin came with him, landing flat on his face while Tzrg managed to land on his feet.

Tzrg slid down a few feet and sheathed his dagger. He took the javelin in both hands and drove it into the Cavemouth goblin's back. The enemy goblin twitched once and was dead. The sight didn't please Tzrg. There was no going back now that Cavemouth blood had been spilled. There was a war on, and it was a war that no one but Rezrex wanted. Though he had accepted the fact that he wasn't as smart as Rezrex and so wasn't sure he'd ever understand why Rezrex would start a war with the Cavemouth Tribe, Tzrg was curious. The idea that a different hobgoblin, an enemy of Rezrex's, had taken over the Cavemouth Tribe had occurred to Tzrg. Then there was the idea that maybe Rezrex wanted the Stonedeep Tribe to have all the vast caves for themselves. Or maybe he was just setting the two goblin tribes against each other for fun, just to see who would win.

Working hard not to slip on the blood-slick stone, Tzrg turned back and was soon face-to-face with Rezrex. Tzrg met the hobgoblin's gaze for just a second before looking down. Rezrex barked out something in the hobgoblin language. Tzrg didn't understand that complex, strange tongue, and he wasn't sure if Rezrex was scolding or congratulating him. Tzrg just kept his mouth shut.

Rezrex laughed, pulled a young goblin warrior up, and waved him into the tunnel. A few more goblins followed, then Rezrex, the last couple goblins, and Tzrg took up the rear. As they passed him, Tzrg could see the fear and confusion on the faces of the goblins. They didn't know what Rezrex had in mind for them either, and they were afraid they were going to find out the hard way, as if they hadn't already.

Tzrg was no better with numbers than any goblin, but he was smart enough to count to eighteen. By his count, only three Cavemouth goblins were dead, and already, thanks to Rezrex, more than three Stonedeep goblins had spilled their lives on a cave floor for the hobgoblin's mysterious cause. Though both tribes had more than eighteen goblins, Tzrg was pretty sure that the Cavemouth Tribe was the bigger of the two.

Rezrex was sending them out to be killed, leaving fewer goblins back in the home caves to protect the females, the young, and the hive spider queen.

What was the most confusing part of the whole thing for Tzrg was the fact that the Stonedeep Tribe was as rich as Tzrg could imagine a goblin tribe being. They had a healthy, happy hive spider queen, who kept her drones obedient and plentiful. The goblins always had enough spider meat to eat, and the drones hunted and gathered cave beetles, blind fish, and other delicacies. The caves were secure, with no tunnels leading deeper and only one way up into Cavemouth territory. The Cavemouth Tribe provided a buffer against any incursions from the surface, and the Stonedeep Tribe stayed home, deep underground with their hive spiders, ate well, made little goblins, and took good care of their caves.

Tzrg, deep in thought, had let himself fall behind. When the first sounds of battle echoed around him from behind the Border Sink waterfall above, his blood ran cold. He stopped, listening to metal clang against metal, bones crack, goblins scream and die, and

Rezrex shout orders in his oddly accented Goblin. The sounds echoed in the tight confines of the shaft until they made Tzrg's ears ring. The goblin was sure he could hear the screams of females.

Tzrg took a deep breath, tightened his grip on his javelin, and joined the fray.

I

"**We've made good time,**" Regdar said, turning to look at Jozan. "The village should be just over this next hill, and we have a few hours of daylight left."

The priest nodded.

"We could continue on," Regdar suggested, "camp along the road."

Jozan patted the neck of his dappled mare and smiled. "They warned me about you in Lianne," the priest said.

Regdar felt his hackles raise. "They warned you about me, Father?"

Jozan coughed out a laugh and said, "They told me you liked to do things the hard way."

"Did they?" Regdar asked.

He was not amused. Regdar didn't think he chose one "way" or another. There was little to fear along the road west from the frontier town of Lianne to the city of New Koratia. How hard could one night outside the confining walls of a smelly old inn be? Regdar slowed his horse and looked over at the priest. Jozan's polished scale mail glinted in the sun, a heavy mace—a real weapon, Regdar was pleased to note—hung from the side of his saddle. Around his neck, strung on thick twine, hung a wooden carving of a stern-faced sun—the symbol of Pelor.

There was something about this priest that Regdar liked. Maybe it was the fact that Jozan looked more like a soldier than a priest, or maybe it was that he was closer to Regdar's own age than any man of the cloth Regdar had ever met. After six years in the Duke's infantry, escorting a lone priest of Pelor—the god Regdar most honored himself—was easy duty. Regdar didn't feel like someone was standing just over the next hill waiting to kill him. He wasn't thinking about the tragedy that had sent him into the army in the first place. He was just riding west through good, clean, hilly country on a good horse, with good company.

The hard way indeed.

"What else did they tell you about me?" Regdar asked.

"They said you know how to use that gigantic sword of yours," Jozan said.

Regdar shrugged, feeling the weight of his greatsword shift on his back. Of course he knew how to use his weapon. He was a soldier.

"They also told me you don't talk much," the priest went on, "and that you don't have many friends."

Regdar looked over at the priest sharply enough to startle his own horse. He had to turn his attention to calming his mount, so couldn't see the priest's reaction. Regdar felt sweat drip from his forehead. It was hot, and his own suit of scale armor was getting heavier. The horse was sweating too, and tired. It was a strong animal, but Regdar, in full armor and with all his gear, was a heavy load.

"Fine, then," Regdar said, "we'll stop at Fairbye for the night."

They came up over the top of the hill riding side by side, and

Regdar could see the little hamlet of Fairbye nestled in the valley below. There were only a couple dozen buildings in all, mostly small wattle-and-daub houses. The village was surrounded by modest fields, vegetable gardens chiefly. A herd of sheep dotted the fields on the other side of town, where the hills started getting bigger as they stacked up against the feet of the high mountains beyond. After a night in Fairbye it would be another day on the road to the entrance to Two Winds Pass, another three days or so across the mountains, then half a day to cross the fields outlying New Koratia.

Regdar snapped his reins and, Jozan behind him, rode at a slow run toward the little village.

Before they even passed the first outlying buildings and turned onto the main street of the town, it became apparent to Regdar that they'd ridden into the middle of something.

"Festival?" he asked Jozan.

The priest rode up next to him, and they both slowed their horses.

"Perhaps," Jozan said. "It looks like the whole town has come out for something."

A handful of shops and a surprisingly large inn were clustered around an ill-defined town square. In the center was a large communal well and a crowd of peasants numbering almost a hundred. Regdar thought Jozan was right when he said that the whole town had come out. The crowd had as many women as men, some quite old, and no shortage of children of all ages. They were all dressed in the simple homespun clothes of the peasantry, and most of the men were holding various farming implements.

Something about the crowd's attitude made Regdar uncomfortable, and he could feel Jozan's unease as well.

"I don't think this is a festival," the priest said, just loudly enough so that only Regdar could hear him.

The fighter nodded and stiffened in his saddle. He wanted to draw his sword, even dismount in order to be ready for whatever was about to happen but was smart enough to know that riding into this sort of scene with naked steel might only make things worse. Still, he could feel his skin tingle and his senses hum with heightened attention.

The villagers were all facing the same direction and listening to a voice still too distant for Regdar to make out. He quickened his horse's pace and heard the word "... guilty!" followed by a rousing cheer from the assembled villagers.

The peasants were facing a crudely constructed gallows on which stood a rotund man dressed in a shimmering silk coat. The man was sweating profusely in the afternoon sun, his hair wet and unkempt. Though the coat was expensive and well tailored, it was obviously old and made to fit a much smaller man. A little girl was standing next to him. Regdar could barely see her head sticking out over the heads of the crowd.

"Hang the bitch!" an old woman shrieked—answered by another ear-ringing cheer from the mob.

"The little girl?" Regdar said, turning to Jozan and beginning to reach for his greatsword.

The priest held up a hand, and Regdar stopped.

"That's no child," Jozan said. "They mean to hang a halfling."

Regdar turned back to the gallows, and as he moved closer still he saw that Jozan was right. Standing next to the portly orator was a halfling woman whose tiny build made her look like a human child. She wore elaborate leathers and had her long, auburn hair tied tightly back. Her hands were bound behind her, and a noose dangled limply from around her neck and was tied to the top of the gallows.

The fat man strutted back and forth on the platform in front of her, waving his hands in an attempt to quiet the still-cheering crowd.

"Good citizens!" the man shouted, and the crowd quieted just enough to hear him. "Good neighbors, we are not murderers here. The halfling woman who calls herself Lidda has been accused of thievery of a most egregious sort—one count after another—"

"What's a count?" a man yelled from the crowd.

This brought about another round of cheering from the assembly, and it took long enough for the round man to quiet them that Regdar and Jozan were able to ride to the edge of the crowd. Only a few people on the edges of the mob noticed them, but they all recognized Jozan as a priest of Pelor and bowed to him in the accepted manner.

Lidda rolled her eyes, and Regdar was amazed at how relaxed she seemed. He got the distinct impression that the woman had been in this situation before.

The crowd quieted a bit, and the fat man was just about to say something when the halfling called out in a clear, unwavering voice, "I will devote my life to finding the true thief. I will clear my name and the names of my family and friends, the names of my acquaintances both personal and professional, and will endeavor to repair any damage done to this fair hamlet by the heinous deeds of this brazen criminal. This I swear, by the three heads of the hydra at the center of the stars!"

Regdar felt his breath catch in his throat and realized that the whole mob was similarly silenced. The halfling was glancing from villager to villager, moving only her wide, nimble eyes.

"Oh," another old woman growled, "let her swing already!"

There was a burst of laughter and applause from the mob, and the fat man in the old coat threw up his hands, his chubby fingers wrapped into tight little fists.

"What are the charges?" Jozan asked in a voice just loud enough to be heard over the crowd.

The rotund orator stopped just before shouting some order or proclamation, and when his eyes found Jozan, he visibly reeled. The man almost fell on his face in his rush to bow, and Regdar watched as every head in the unruly mob turned to look at Jozan.

Regdar was horrified by the sudden attention of the lynch mob, and his hand went to the pommel of his greatsword. He was convinced the villagers would turn on them, but they froze, all eyes glued to the priest. Most of them sketched slight bows and whispered to each other that Pelor had sent a priest to bless the hanging. Regdar doubted that was the case. He took his hand off his sword.

"The charges?" Jozan asked again.

The fat man, obviously flustered, called out, "A priest of Pelor! Come to bless today's justice!"

The crowd applauded but with a measure of reluctance this time.

Jozan called back, "Pelor does not bless lynchings, Mister . . . ?"

"I am the burgher here, Father," the fat man replied. "Tomma is the name, sir."

Jozan rode forward slowly, the crowd parting before him. Regdar stood his ground and seemed to go largely unnoticed by the villagers.

"What has this woman done," the priest asked, "to deserve a death sentence, Burgher Tomma?"

"Ah," the burgher replied, obviously delighted to recount the charges. "The halfling has stolen numerous items of personal property from numerous goodly townsfolk and farmers on numerous occasions, good priest . . . ?"

"Jozan," the priest said. "But that you could hang her numerous times then, Burgher."

The crowd was split as to whether or not to cheer that, and the resulting confusion made Regdar smile.

"Thank you, Father," Lidda said. "Maybe you could just smash my head in with your mace and get it over with."

A man in the crowd shouted, "Do it, Father!"

A few of the women gasped, and Jozan turned on the man, his face a cold mask. Regdar had never seen Jozan look like that before. The priest was more than angry, he was mortified—struck momentarily dumb with rage.

"Um . . ." the burgher said.

"There is a justice in the world," Jozan said, his voice clear and steady, "that is greater than the rule of the mob. If this woman is guilty of a crime, let her be judged in the proper venue. Let her meet her accusers, and let her have a chance to defend herself before her neck is snapped."

"See," Lidda said to the burgher's back. "I told you you can't just string me up you fat f—"

"Hold your tongue!" Jozan commanded. Regdar was impressed by the fact that the accused did indeed silence herself. "You may still swing, child, if you're as guilty as they—"

"*Help me!*" a wild, panicked voice screamed from the other side of the crowd. The mob of villagers turned, and this time Regdar drew his sword.

The crowd reacted as one, bowing in on one side as if something had struck its edge and bent it back. Regdar, from astride his horse, could see a boy, no older than fifteen, rushing into the crowd and being held on his feet by a pocket of concerned villagers. The boy was a mess, drenched in sweat and covered in dirt. His clothes were torn, and he held the broken half of a shepherd's staff.

"Spiders!" the shepherd cried.

Regdar slipped off his horse, scanning all around for any sign of whatever it was the boy was afraid of—spiders or otherwise. He saw nothing threatening, and for safety's sake he sheathed his sword before he got to the boy's side. Regdar reached out and helped a few of the villagers lower the shepherd to sit on the hard-packed dirt of the village square.

"Get him some water," Regdar said to one of the villagers, a young woman who appeared to have her wits about her while the others were still caught up in the tensions of the moment.

The woman rushed off for water, and Regdar crouched next to the shepherd. There was a disturbance in the crowd, and Jozan pushed through the parting farmers to join Regdar at the boy's side.

"Is he injured?" the priest asked.

Regdar examined the boy quickly and saw no blood or any sign of injury beyond a few scrapes. Jozan was looking at the boy even more closely, so Regdar didn't bother to answer.

"Spiders," the boy gasped, not looking at anyone in particular. "Big, huge, brown spiders . . . I've never even heard of spiders that big."

"Are you injured, son?" Jozan asked. "Were you bitten by any of these spiders?"

The boy blinked and met Jozan's steady gaze. He was shaking. "Am I dead? Are you Pelor?"

"Hey!" the halfling called. "Can I go now?"

The crowd responded by screaming "No!" at the top of their lungs. Regdar's attention was torn between the mob and the shepherd.

"No, son," Jozan told the boy, "I'm not Pelor. Just a humble priest anxious to hear your tale."

"Spiders," the boy repeated without pause. "They attacked the sheep. They bit one apart and dragged it away in pieces, then more came and attacked another one . . . and I got the hell ou—sorry, Father. I ran away. I don't think they were chasing me. I can't . . . I can't . . ."

The boy began panting, hyperventilating.

The fat burgher came through the crowd, a pungent stench following him, and he rushed to the boy's side. "Gürn," he said. "Gürn, my son, is the flock safe?"

"Poppa?" the boy replied, though he could hardly breathe.

Burgher Tomma put a hand on the boy's shoulder and asked, "Is the flock safe, son? Are the sheep safe?"

"Big . . . giant . . . spiders . . . attacked them," Gürn answered. "I don't know how many were . . . taken."

"You let them—" Tomma gasped, his pudgy face draining of color so that Regdar thought they'd need to send someone for water for the burgher.

The woman appeared with a cup of water and handed it to the shaking boy. Burgher Tomma took it from his son and drank it down greedily, the fat man gasping for air along with his son.

"Not the sheep," he said. He looked up at Jozan, his eyes pleading. "The sheep are our whole lives. Without them, we have nothing. The whole village depends on them."

Gasps and whispers pulsed through the mob in waves, and Regdar watched all their faces go as pale as the burgher's. Regdar had been to villages like this one—villages that depended on one herd of livestock or one field of crops for their entire existence.

"Regdar," Jozan said, "have you heard of spiders big enough to carry off a sheep?"

Regdar nodded and said, "I've heard tales, but I've never seen one."

Jozan stood and turned all the way around, scanning the crowd. "Are you expected in New Koratia?" he asked Regdar.

Regdar shrugged. "I had intended to see my mother," he said, "but she wouldn't know when to expect me. Why?"

"Burgher Tomma," Jozan said, "we'll see to these spiders for you."

The fat man sagged with relief, and his eyes puffed and filled with tears. "Oh . . . oh, Father. How can we ever thank you . . . you and your man . . . ?"

Regdar wasn't quite sure what he was hearing, but it sounded suspiciously like he had just volunteered to ride off after giant spiders to save someone else's sheep. The crowd appeared horrified and relieved at the same time, and none of them looked like any use in a fight.

"We'll take the halfling with us as well," Jozan told the burgher.

The fat man looked at him as if the priest had suddenly sprouted green fur and a bug's antennae.

"It will afford me an opportunity to question her thoroughly," Jozan said. "Otherwise I will have to question her here and deal with your spider problem in a few days' time."

"Take her," Burgher Tomma gasped, forcing a smile. "For Pelor's sake, take her."

"Yeah," Lidda called from the gallows, "let's go get those spiders, darn it. I love sheep."

Naull ran a hand through her short, straight hair and sighed. She had prepared the spell that morning, along with four others, and it was a simple matter of tracing a pattern in the air in front of her with one finger while whispering a series of arcane syllables to make the magic real. She sat at a rough oak table in the dining room of her mentor's tower and let the magical energies flow through her fingers, through the words that slipped off her tongue, and onto the leather pouch on the table in front of her.

There was no flash of lightning or explosion of fire, but Naull could see the air over the table sparkle for the space of maybe the blink of an eye. There was a wide tear in the bottom of the old pouch, and as the sparkles faded, the tear closed. In the time it took for Naull to draw in a single breath, the pouch, which her mentor had assured her was older than Naull herself, looked as if it had been newly made.

She clicked her teeth together and looked over at the little room's only window. It wasn't really so much a window as an arrow loop—a thin, vertical sliver of light no wider than one of Naull's slender hands. It was sunny outside, still a few hours before dark. She heard wind blowing through leaves beyond but couldn't see the trees. The dining room was a good hundred feet up the tall, slender tower that was the secluded home of her mentor, the wizard Larktiss Dathient.

Naull stood and crossed to the window. She peered through the thin opening and out into the warm air. Below were the well-manicured gardens that kept her busy in the spring and fall. Beyond was a small forest, rolling hills, and the world she had seen so little of in her eighteen years.

The fresh air felt good, at least, and made her feel less sleepy. She knew she shouldn't be tired, but boredom could do that to you, and Naull was crushingly bored. She rubbed her stiff neck, and her hand brushed her right ear. This made her realize that she hadn't put on her earrings that morning. Her hair was cut short, well above her shoulders because it was easier to take care of and didn't get in the way of her spellcasting and other duties. She wore a man's tunic and breeches for the same reason.

The window faced west, and she knew that somewhere over the horizon was the city of New Koratia. She might look ridiculous there with her boy's haircut and man's clothes, but at least there would be something to do there, people and things to see, some kind of life not limited to learning how to use something she was never permitted to use. There might be—there *would* be—men.

She heard the door open and didn't turn around.

"Staring out the window again?" Larktiss asked, his voice dripping with overstated disapproval. "I've brought the heavier needle."

Naull pressed her face into the thin arrow loop and said, "It's done already."

She closed her eyes and listened to the old man shuffle over to the table, pick up the magically mended pouch, and throw it back down again.

"There was a reason I asked you to fix it with a needle and thread, Naull," he said.

She took her face off the stone but didn't turn around.

"I want to leave," she said.

"We're going to have this conversation again, then, are we?" the old man asked.

Naull turned to him, and her hands went to her hips. She started to say, "Larktiss—"

Her tone made her feel instantly guilty, and she took her hands from her hips and shook her fingers to keep from clenching them into fists.

"You're not a prisoner here, child," Larktiss said. "You know you never have been, and you never will be."

"I don't want to just leave, Larktiss. I want you to understand why I have to go." She looked at the floor. "I want your blessing."

"And you'll have it," he replied, "in due time."

Naull couldn't stop her hands from curling into fists, but she kept her arms at her sides. "I have been a good student," she said. "I've done everything you've ever asked me to do. I can't stay here forever."

The old man smiled, showing yellow teeth. His face was as kindly as ever, and though Naull usually found his easy manner and deeply lined, wise face comforting, sometimes she thought he looked like the world's kindliest jailer. His white hair—what was left of it—was as disheveled as always, but his long, brown robe was immaculately clean. Naull returned his smile.

"I never said you had to stay here forever, Naull," Larktiss said. "I do wish I could tell you precisely how much longer you should stay, but magic is not an exact science. It's more an art. You have learned the most basic elements of the craft, but you lack both experience and an understanding of the nuances. A young mage with your limited abilities and your seemingly limitless self-confidence—" with this his smile was gone all together, and his soft face went hard—"could be more dangerous than—"

"If I lack experience," Naull interrupted, "it's because I've hardly left this damned tower in the last six years. I have learned your lessons and mended your pouches and darned your socks and fetched the water. . . . Is that the sort of experience you had in mind?"

The old man looked disappointed, and Naull had to look at the floor again.

"I don't want to hurt you, Larktiss," she said, "and I don't want to defy you. You have taught me well and treated me better. I don't know where I would be if you hadn't taken me in. I owe you more than I will ever be able to repay, but . . ."

"But your wisdom has outgrown mine," he said, his voice unusually weak.

She looked at him and sighed. "No, Larktiss, my wisdom hasn't outgrown yours, my . . . curiosity . . . ambition . . . I don't know. I have outgrown this place. I need to be around more than one person, for Boccob's sake."

"I know," he said, looking at the floor the same way Naull had. "I have had other students. They have always come to me, just like you, and told me that it was time for them to leave. I let them go, the same way I suppose I'll let you go. At first it was because I thought they were right, then because I couldn't convince them that I was right. Either way, they left to see the world and experience its wonders and dangers. I watched all of them from here, unable to do anything but observe."

The old man stopped talking and stood. Naull could hear his old joints creak. He looked at her with sadness drawing the corners of his eyes down. Naull felt her eyes fill with tears.

"I've had twenty students," Larktiss continued, "including you. Do you know how many of them are still alive?"

Naull didn't answer.

"You," he said. "Only you."

She drew in a breath and stood there, arms at her sides, a single tear rolling down one cheek.

The old man sighed so heavily it was as if all the air rushed out of him at once. He seemed to deflate in front of her. Naull almost reached out to steady him but didn't.

He looked at her with an obviously forced smile and asked, "Where will you go?"

She had to clear her throat, then pause for a moment before she could say, "Fairbye, to start, I suppose. I can pick up the trade road from there to New Koratia and beyond."

The old man nodded and said, "Beyond. . . ."

"I have no intention of getting myself killed," she said.

The old man shrugged. "Of course you don't," he said. "You're a good little mage, Naull, and with luck you might live to be great one, but there is something you need to understand."

Naull waited while Larktiss struggled with what he felt he had to say next.

"If you leave here before I believe you're ready," he said finally, "you will not be welcomed back."

Naull sniffed, wiped the tears from her face, and said, "Like hell, old man. I'll be back to visit you every year, no matter what life hands me, no matter where I end up."

The old man nodded, but his eyes were distant. Naull understood that he believed it wouldn't matter if she was welcomed or not or intended to return or not. He was sure he would never see her again.

"Fairbye," he said, crossing slowly, stiffly to the door. "You'll need some things. I can give you pouches—you'll need pouches, you know, for spell components, and—"

He stopped talking so he could keep himself from crying. After a moment, he opened the door.

"Get dressed," said the old man. "I can spare a backpack, I think, and a torch or three. Don't forget your spellbook." He turned to face her, his face serious, his eyes red. "Never, ever forget your spellbook, girl. It is a mage's—"

"Life," she finished for him. She'd heard him say it enough. "It's a mage's life."

He smiled weakly and walked through the door. She listened to his shuffling footsteps recede for a minute, then took the pouch from the table and left the room herself.

Larktiss had gone down the steep spiral stairs that ran up the center of the cylindrical tower. Naull went up. She took the steps two at a time—a habit that always annoyed and worried Larktiss—and was through the door into her cramped bedchamber in less than a minute.

She scanned the room quickly, having worked out long ago what she would take with her when she left. There was the crossbow and a quiver of quarrels, a flint and steel, her long, straight quarterstaff. She scooped up the earrings that were all she had left of her mother and put them on. They were heavy, jagged things that only accentuated her boyish haircut, but they were her only possession of any real value.

She stripped out of her work clothes and slid on a pair of beige harem pants she'd sewn herself and never worn, then a long-sleeved, corseted top and a stiff leather riding hood. There was a tall mirror in her room, and she looked at herself. She looked like a traveler, a pilgrim, a wanderer, an adventurer. She looked like anything but a sheltered girl bent to endless study.

She smiled and, taking her staff, turned and walked out of the room she'd called her own for six years without looking back. If she'd thought about it, she might have spent a moment or two soaking in the sights and smells of the tower as she made her way down the long spiral stairs. Instead, she took the stairs practically at a run and almost bowled her aging mentor over when they emptied out onto the ground floor of the tower.

"At least have the good manners not to appear to be in such a gods-bedamned hurry, girl," Larktiss said, sincerely annoyed.

Naull took a deep breath and steadied herself. The old man held up a strap of old, threadbare pouches. He nodded, and she tipped her head down to let him drape them over her shoulder. The bandoleer was surprisingly light, the leather soft with age. She straightened and forced a smile.

In his other hand he held a little leather sack, bunched together at the top and tied. He handed it to her, and she took it, surprised by the weight.

"A few coins," he said, then nodded to a backpack on the floor at her feet.

Naull smiled and said, "Larktiss . . ."

"Bah," the old man scoffed, waving a hand at her. "Don't get too excited, girl, they're mostly coppers . . . but they'll get you started if you stay clear of thieves and avoid the finer things in life."

Naull laughed, and Larktiss looked away. She was sure she saw the old man smile. He turned and opened the door, letting in the bright late afternoon sun and the warm, muggy air. Naull bent and grabbed the backpack, slipping it around her shoulders. It was heavy.

Her mentor waved her out the door, avoiding her eyes as she passed. She stopped in the doorway to give him a kiss on the cheek. He did smile then, and patted her on the shoulder the way he always did when he didn't know what else to do.

"Farewell, Larktiss," Naull said, stepping out of the tower into the wide world.

He said nothing, just closed the door behind her.

Regdar crouched and ran a finger over the dry grass. When he drew his hand back, the tips of his fingers were stained with blood.

"Sheep?" Jozan asked him.

Regdar looked up at the priest, grunted, and said, "You over-estimate my abilities as a tracker."

Jozan smiled and nodded. "This is the place the shepherd boy described?"

Regdar stood. "Something was killed here," he said, "and recently."

He looked around again and saw no sign of giant spiders, though there were dozens of sheep wandering the short, drought-stunted grass on the side of the hill.

"Very good, Randar," Lidda said. "So, everything's fine here." She clapped her hands once and took a step back away from the two heavily armored men. "The spiders are gone, and the sheep look fine. So, thanks for everything, but—"

"My name is Regdar," Regdar cut in. "And you will be free to go when Jozan says you're free to go. If you pretend to not understand that, I will be forced to—"

"Easy there, big fella," she sneered, "you're sweeping me off my—"

"That'll be all," Jozan interrupted in turn, glancing at Regdar, "from both of you. Let us assume that what the shepherd boy said was true and that a sheep was attacked and killed here. He said it was dragged off . . . in which direction?"

Regdar looked back at the ground and said, "There'll be a trail of blood. It hasn't rained, so the blood wasn't washed away, but it has soaked into the dry grass." He held up his bloodstained fingers.

"So once again, Pelor shows us that the path to enlightenment is best traveled on our knees," Jozan said. He knelt as quickly as his stiff armor allowed and began to pass his hands over the brown grass. "We may not be able to see the blood trail, but we can feel it."

Regdar lowered himself to his knees near where he'd found the first bit of blood. He passed his hands over the ground in front of him the same as Jozan and soon found the patch of blood-soaked grass. In a less than a minute, he had determined a rough perimeter of where the sheep was initially attacked and was reasonably sure he knew in which direction it was dragged.

"It's this way, Jozan," he said. "Find anything, Lidda?"

There was no answer, and Jozan said, "Lidda?"

Regdar looked around and saw Jozan do the same thing. The halfling woman was gone.

Regdar drew his greatsword from his back and ran in one direction while Jozan ran in the other. They both knew she wouldn't go back to Fairbye, so they didn't bother looking for her that way. The hills made it hard to see very far, and there was the odd copse of trees here and there and in one direction, the edge of a proper forest.

Regdar had never been trained to hide, but he had been trained to seek. He scanned the shadows under the trees for any movement and the underbrush for signs of anything bigger than a squirrel. He kept moving the whole time. She'd been gone for a couple minutes, no more, but a fast little halfling, who was most likely a thief just like the people of Fairbye thought, could get far in a couple minutes.

"Anything?" he called out to Jozan.

"She's gone," Jozan answered. "Never mind. Let her go."

Regdar turned around, and it was all he could do to keep from sprinting in Jozan's direction. He hadn't known the priest long, but he knew Jozan wouldn't decide to stop looking for the halfling. Though Regdar wasn't sure what the priest was trying to tell him, it was obvious that Regdar was looking in the wrong direction.

He was nearly at Jozan's side when the priest waved him off. Regdar met the other man's gaze, and Jozan nodded once, then moved his eyes slowly to one side without turning his head. Regdar resisted the temptation to look in the direction Jozan had indicated. Instead, he sheathed his sword and bent to one knee.

Regdar touched the ground and said, "Good riddance to bad company, then. I'll find the trail again, and we'll get on with it."

The fighter tensed his legs, ready to spring forward into a run, and Jozan took a few steps backward, but in the direction he'd indicated with his eyes. There was a sheep a few yards from him, grazing at the dry grass, as oblivious as one would expect a sheep to be. It was grazing near the edge of a copse of trees that were being choked by a dense mat of underbrush—tall bushes with brilliant yellow flowers. The branches were dense enough, and the shadows dark enough to hide a halfling.

Jozan whispered something, and Regdar was about to ask him to repeat himself when the priest looked up and shouted, "*Scream!*"

in a voice that made gooseflesh burst up on the undersides of Regdar's arms.

The command was followed immediately by a loud, shrill scream like a little girl's. It was coming from the underbrush, and Regdar leaped to his feet, counting off the seconds to himself.

. . . two . . .

Under the scream he heard footsteps, light and close together, and receding.

. . . three . . .

He led the sound of the halfling's feet and launched himself over the first row of yellow bushes.

. . . four . . .

He saw the side of her face whip past the trunk of a tree and turned so he would come up just behind her.

. . . five . . .

She stopped and swerved on one heel with a lithe grace Regdar had to admire even as he was cursing it. He practically fell sideways to compensate.

. . . six . . .

She stopped screaming and dived for cover behind another tree, but Regdar's hand came down and took up a handful of her long, carefully braided hair.

Lidda jumped toward him. It was exactly what Regdar would have done if he was in her place, so he knew how and when to take advantage of it. There was a flash of steel, and Regdar brought his other hand up past his chest and batted the hand Lidda was holding the dagger in away from his throat. The weapon went sailing, and Lidda gasped in pain and surprise.

Regdar slipped a hand around her waist and turned her around to face him. He took his hand from her hair and wrapped it around the pommel of her sheathed short sword.

And to think, he hadn't stopped Jozan from talking the towns-people into giving her her weapons back.

She tried once to squirm out of his grip, but when he squeezed her she stopped.

"Yeah, well, all right, then," she said, not breathing as hard as Regdar would have expected. "Watch the spiky bits, there, Ramdor."

He dropped her to her feet, careful not to snag her on any of his armor's spikes. Regdar slid his right arm around to under her arm and back behind her head. His left hand stayed on her sword. She must have known how easy it would be for him to break her neck, so she didn't try to get away. Jozan approached, having some trouble moving through the undergrowth. Regdar dropped to one knee, so he wasn't improperly balanced, leaning over the halfling who was only half his height.

Lidda turned her head enough to see Jozan and said, "Yeah, like that was fair. Your god actually lets you do that sort of thing to an innocent girl just trying to see a little of the world?"

"Pelor," Jozan said, smiling, "moves in mysterious ways."

Lidda opened her mouth to speak again but stopped herself. Regdar figured even she was smart enough to know that you can insult a priest, but you better think twice before insulting his god.

Tzrg gripped the tray with both hands and eyed the slippery surface of the flowstone ledge. Rezrex and two of his hobgoblins sat near the edge, tossing loose stones off the high drop-off—as tall as thirteen or fourteen goblins—into the normally mirror-still water of the big crystal pool below. The hobgoblins looked angular and brutal against the smooth, rounded white surface of the flowstone.

"Beer!" the big hobgoblin shouted, waving Tzrg forward.

Tzrg didn't used to serve beer. It was a female's job before Rezrex came and should have been a female's job afterward. Rezrex didn't like the female goblins coming near him, though. He said things about them in the hobgoblin language that Tzrg didn't understand. Rezrex had killed a total of twelve of the Stonedeep goblins—either himself, one of his other hobgoblins, or in battle against the Cavemouth Tribe—but none of them female. It meant the Stonedeep Tribe might still have a future, but either way it would be a future created for them by Rezrex.

A single harsh word in the hobgoblin tongue echoed against the ceiling some hundred feet up. Tzrg jumped. It was Rezrex who had shouted, because Tzrg wasn't bringing the beer fast enough.

With three heavy stone flagons full of beer on it, the tray was heavy. It wasn't easy for Tzrg to carry it without spilling, and he knew he'd be punished if he spilled. He walked carefully, not looking over the edge, and managed to get within the huge hobgoblin's reach without spilling any of the bitter fungus beer.

Rezrex's face twisted into a hideous, huge grin, showing ragged yellow fangs and diseased gums. Tzrg looked away before he made eye contact. He looked down and felt Rezrex take one of the flagons from the slate tray. As the other two hobgoblins took their drinks, Tzrg's eyes wandered to the cave behind where Rezrex was sitting on a carved stone chair. Behind Rezrex and to Tzrg's left was the dark, round entrance to the side-passage that was once Tzrg's private cave. It was the cave that all the chiefs of the Stonedeep Tribe had lived in for generation after generation. Tzrg hadn't seen the inside of it in weeks.

Rezrex said something in the hobgoblin language, but the only word Tzrg recognized was what he had come to think of as Rezrex's nickname for him. Tzrg didn't know exactly what the word meant, but he was pretty sure it was an insult. He'd never heard Rezrex use it to refer to anyone else.

Tzrg looked up and saw that Rezrex was looking at him expectantly, as if he was waiting for the goblin to respond. Tzrg had been in this situation more than once with Rezrex and usually, he just said "*Tzrg pzvmp.*"—Tzrg serves.

This time, though, the words caught in Tzrg's throat. There were a dozen goblins in the deep shadows off to his right and back, away from the hobgoblin. They were eyeing the beer barrel, their eyes flicking from it to Tzrg and back again. They wanted beer, but Rezrex was denying them drink. They were limited to water as if they were females, and they didn't like it. They kept looking at Tzrg as if he could do something about it.

Rezrex batted the tray out of Tzrg's hands, and it smashed him in the face. He stepped back and pinwheeled his arms. Behind him was a sheer drop into water Tzrg knew was over his head. He managed not to fall off only by the slightest margin. The tray went spinning down, bouncing off the smooth, pale flowstone, and splashed into the crystal pool.

The two hobgoblins, who sat on either side of Rezrex, laughed hysterically.

"*Kdl Tzrg,*" the hobgoblin growled. "*Kdl Rezrex.*"—Tzrg's cave. Rezrex's cave.

Tzrg couldn't help glancing at the entrance to the little cave that used to mark him as the chief of the Stonedeep Tribe. The goblins who'd been looking to him to get them beer came forward a few steps, craning their necks to see him.

Tzrg had a flash of anger—he was angry at the other goblins, his goblins. They had stepped aside when Rezrex came, hadn't resisted the hobgoblins either. They all looked at him like he was supposed to do something, but none of them were willing to do anything themselves. They went up the cave with Rezrex and raided the Cavemouth Tribe. They even helped to steal the Cavemouth's hive spider queen. They all knew what that meant for the Cavemouth goblins: feral spiders, chaos, death. They helped to shatter the old treaties that kept the Cavemouth Tribe safely up high, and the Stonedeep Tribe safely below. They did what Rezrex told them to do, just like Tzrg, but they still had the nerve to look at him like—

Tzrg was lurched forward so fast and so hard his neck almost snapped. Rezrex was holding him by the front of his ragged tunic, taking up some of Tzrg's chest hair with the mildewed old cloth. Tzrg hissed in pain as he was lifted off his feet and drawn in close to the hobgoblin's huge, stinking face.

"Listen, Tzrg," Rezrex growled in halting Goblin. "Rezrex leads. More than eighteen goblins. More than eighteen tribes. Rezrex leads. Leads goblins. Tzrg knows?"

Tzrg nodded, letting himself hang there. Tzrg understood what the hobgoblin meant. He was going to lead all the goblins. Every goblin would fall under his leadership. Tzrg couldn't imagine how such a thing might be possible, then he considered the size of the beast that was holding him off the ground with one hand. There was the magical mace, too, and the hobgoblin henchmen . . . and the Stonedeep Tribe. Maybe it wasn't so hard to imagine after all.

It had taken Rezrex less than a week to take complete control of the Stonedeep Tribe. The Cavemouth goblins had resisted, and all that did was get more than eighteen of them killed and the rest thrown into cages to think about the folly of their resistance. Tzrg knew goblins—Stonedeep, Cavemouth, or whatever tribe—well enough to know they'd give in soon enough and give in completely. What else could they to do?

"Tzrg knows," Rezrex said, looking the goblin in the eye.

Tzrg nodded and said, "Tzrg knows."

He was launched backward into the cool cave air. His arms started flapping—he couldn't stop them. His stomach jumped up into his chest. Tzrg fell and fell for what seemed like a full minute but wasn't really more than a couple seconds. He hit the water hard—hard enough to smash the air from his lungs and leave him in the freezing cold pool, locked in mid-gasp lest he take in a lungful of water.

When he climbed out of the water, gurgling, desperate for air, Tzrg briefly wondered why he'd bothered to hold his breath. It might have been over.

"**Y'know,**" **Lidda complained,** "all this justice stuff is hurting my knees."

Regdar suppressed a smile and glanced down at the little half-ling. Jozan had seen fit to have Lidda crawl along the dry grass, following the blood trail, and Regdar couldn't help but feel for her. She was certainly a thief, but there was something about her that Regdar found . . . charming? It wasn't a word Regdar used overmuch.

"It goes into the woods, I think," Lidda reported, sitting up on her knees and stretching her back.

Regdar followed her gaze forward to the edge of a deep pine forest that made its way up a particularly steep hill. They'd come easily three hours from Fairbye, and the sun was low over the high mountains in the west. The glaciers sparkled, and the mountains turned purple. Streaks of orange and pink colored the sky.

"Spiders would like the woods," Jozan said. "It's darker in there, and they could spin webs between the trees."

Lidda stood, hugging her arms close to her body. "Yeah, well, mystery solved. Drinks are on me, boys. Last one back to Fairbye is a—"

"Hanged thief?" Jozan finished for her.

Regdar laughed, and Lidda shot him a stern, annoyed look.

"You want to go in there, following giant spiders, to save a sheep? We've been following a trail of its blood for, like, three miles. I don't think the sheep's gonna make it, guys."

"We're not going to save the sheep, Lidda," Regdar said. "We're going to kill the spiders."

"Really?" she asked, looking into the edge of the woods rather than at Regdar. "You might want to start with that one."

Regdar started to say, "What?" but didn't have a chance to before Jozan shouted his name.

The big fighter drew the greatsword from his back with a shriek of steel on steel at the same time he saw the spider creep out from the underbrush at the edge of the woods. He knew that Jozan would have his mace out, and Lidda drew a bolt from her quiver and slid the crossbow from her back. It was impossible for Regdar to tell if the spider was looking at him, or at either of his friends, or at none of them. The thing had eight eyes of different sizes, all black circles that glistened in the sunset.

It came right at Jozan, who happened to be closer to it than either Regdar or Lidda. The priest stepped toward it, hefting his mace, his footsteps firm and confident. Regdar liked what he saw and smiled around gritted teeth.

There was a soft, rubbery sound from behind him—Lidda had fired her crossbow. The bolt shot wide of the spider and burrowed deep into the ground not ten inches from Jozan's foot. The priest sidestepped, and the spider jumped.

Regdar hadn't even seen the spider tense its eight, brown-and-beige striped legs, but the arachnid was in the air as fast as Lidda's bolt. Regdar lunged at the thing almost as quickly, but he knew he wouldn't get to it before it got to Jozan.

The priest let himself fall the rest of the way to the side, and the spider flashed past him. It hit the ground facing away from Jozan, and the priest rolled to his right, kicking out in front of him and to the side to make himself roll faster. The mace came down on the spider's tear-shaped body, and there was a wet cracking sound and a burst of yellow ichor that obscured the medium brown **X**-shaped marking on the spider's back.

Regdar drew himself up short and started to think about whether he should congratulate Jozan on the kill first or chastise Lidda for nearly nailing his friend's foot to the ground. He had just about made a decision when another spider leaped out of the shadows at the edge of the forest and hit him hard on the side.

Regdar staggered back a few steps, and the spider scrambled up his body, its freakish sideways jaws, bristling with coarse fur, snapping at his face. Regdar thought the thing meant to bite his head off. The tiny, but sharp and strong claws at the tips of its segmented legs dug into the seams of his armor, gripping its way up him.

He couldn't get his greatsword in at that angle, so he held it in his left hand and grabbed the huge spider—it was easily eighteen inches around—where its spherical head met its tear-shaped body.

Regdar pushed the thing away, and it came off with three distinct snapping sounds. Three of its claws had hooked so firmly into his armor that when he pulled it off him, the three legs stayed where they were, and the body came away, trailing yellow ooze. The spider started thrashing madly in Regdar's grip, and the fighter wasn't sure he could hold the thing. He squeezed it as hard as he could, but he couldn't snap its neck.

The sound of Lidda's crossbow hummed again, and Regdar was afraid she might be trying to help him. He wasn't sure which he was more afraid of, the spider's jaws or Lidda's wildly flying cross-bow bolts.

"Behind you, Lidda!" Jozan shouted, and all at once Regdar realized that there were more spiders.

It wasn't easy, but he managed to get his greatsword in-between the still thrashing spider he held in his right hand and the side of his body. He punched the tip of the blade through the spider and let go with his right hand. The thing spasmed once, curled its five remaining legs in, and slid off the end of his blade, dead.

The ground all around Regdar was scattered with more of the fast-moving beige bodies. He kicked one, sending it into the air between Lidda and Jozan—directly into the path of one of Lidda's steel bolts. The spider seemed to hang in the air for a second before changing direction an inch or so and falling dead to the ground. The crossbow bolt might have hit Jozan if Regdar hadn't inadvertently lobbed a spider into the air between them.

Regdar stepped back to avoid one spider, and another bit him on the calf, through the hard leather of his boots. The fangs stung going in and held on tight, pinching him. He felt his own blood burst into his boot and soak his calf. With a curse, he hacked down hard and sliced the spider cleanly in two. A wave of hot yellow gore washed over his legs, and the spider's bite released.

He managed to stay on his feet and turned to see Jozan strike at a spider on the ground, but the thing dodged away, moving perfectly sideways. Lidda was running backward, her knees popping up almost to the level of her chin as she danced away from the clattering mandibles of five spiders.

Regdar stomped down on another spider at his feet. His heavy heel came down right in the middle of the big **X** on the spider's back. The carapace cracked, and the spider scuttled away, wounded but alive.

Jozan was fighting a bizarre duel with one spider, and Lidda screamed in frustration and fear. Regdar spun and lifted one foot to close with the five spiders that were harrying the halfling. He wasn't able to finish that step before the dwindling early evening light was washed away by a spray of multicolored lightning.

Regdar put an arm up to block his eyes. Every color of the rainbow wrapped itself into a cone of dazzling brilliance that bathed the spiders in front of Lidda. The creatures scattered and tumbled along the ground, and Lidda fell hard on her nicely rounded behind. The short sword she'd been trying so hard to draw came out of its scabbard all at once and reflected the green, yellow, orange, purple, and white light.

Then the colored light was gone, and Regdar moved fast toward Lidda. The halfling was sitting on the ground, bringing her short sword in front of her and waving it uncertainly at the spiders lying motionless in front of her. The things looked dead.

A loud *crack!* sounded behind him, and Regdar turned to see that Jozan had finally managed to smash the dueling spider with his mace. The priest was breathing hard, dripping in sticky yellow fluid but otherwise unhurt.

"All right," Lidda gasped, "what's all this then?"

Regdar said, "I don't know."

"It was a color spray," a voice said. All three whirled to face a young woman who was walking slowly toward them. "It worked nicely, didn't it? Nuance my a—"

"Who are you?" Regdar demanded, stepping toward her.

The woman stopped and put up both hands as if to ward him off, though the fighter was still a good ten paces from her.

"It's all right," she said.

"You did that?" Lidda asked, standing. She was obviously trying to look at the newcomer but was having a hard time keeping her eyes off the spiders. "You killed them."

"You cast a spell," Jozan said, stepping up next to Regdar. "A well timed and well executed one at that, I must say. We all three owe you thanks. Young Lidda in particular."

Lidda sheathed her unused sword and started dusting herself off. All three of them looked a mess. The halfling had a strange expression on her face. She looked angry, somehow, maybe frustrated.

Regdar ignored her moods and turned to the young woman. She was pretty, and Regdar rarely thought that about women. For a soldier women were just . . . well, it wasn't possible to be married and fight for the duke, so he always assumed that would come later, after he retired.

Regdar actually shook his head. Where were these thoughts coming from all of a sudden?

"I'm Jozan," the priest said, "a cleric in the service of Pelor. My traveling companion here is Regdar, who served the Duke of Koratia and now serves the temple as well, and—"

"I know my own name," Lidda said, "thank you, Jozan."

The halfling approached the young woman stiffly, reluctantly, and held out her tiny hand. The stranger leaned over and returned the handshake.

"Lidda," the halfling said, "and I owe you one—*damn it!*"

The young woman was as confused by the outburst as Regdar and Jozan were, but she managed to say, "Naull. My name is Naull."

Regdar repeated the name in his head: Naull. He found himself smiling, and when Naull looked up at him, all he could do was bow.

"They're not dead," Naull said, glancing between all three of them.

Lidda turned around, backing up almost into the young woman. The halfling regarded the motionless spiders with a grimace and said, "They aren't?"

Regdar tightened his grip on his sword and looked at the

spiders. They appeared dead from where he was standing.

"The spell just kind of knocks them out for a few minutes," Naull explained. "When they wake up, they'll be blind and kind of stunned. That only lasts another few minutes as well, then they'll be back to normal, and likely none too happy."

Regdar looked at her, and she shrugged, half smiling at him. He wasn't sure what to say.

"What do you mean 'a few minutes'?" asked Lidda.

Naull shrugged, looking a bit embarrassed. "Well, it's not an exact science, but if you want to kill them, you should get on with it."

Regdar and Jozan needed no further prompting. They made absolutely certain that each of the five stunned spiders were cut into at least two pieces or smashed as flat as parchment. Lidda refused to look, and Naull turned almost as many colors as the light from her spell.

"Done?" Lidda asked after the sounds of cracking carapaces stopped, not turning to look.

"Done," Regdar told her.

"Good," the halfling said. "Let's go wash up and get a good night's sleep."

"We're not done, Lidda," Jozan said.

"Oh, come on!" Lidda said, stomping her foot.

"You're looking for where they came from," Naull said.

Regdar raised an eyebrow and met the slim woman's warm gaze. "Would you happen to know that?" he asked.

"Me?" answered Naull. "Oh, no, sorry. I've never seen spiders like this before. I was just on my way to Fairbye when I heard all the shouting and scuffling around."

"Well," Jozan broke in, "you're right, anyway. We will need to find the source of these spiders. . . . Their lair, if they have one. If you can do that spell again, we'd appreciate the help."

"No!" Lidda answered for her. She turned on the woman and

almost fell to her knees. "Say no. Don't go with them . . . seriously. If you go with them, then I have to go with them because I owe you one now, and I just so do not want to go with these suicidal maniacs. You were going to Fairbye. . . . Let's go to Fairbye."

Naull looked confused, turning to Jozan with silently pleading eyes.

"Lidda forgets that the people of Fairbye were about to string her up," Jozan said, "and will be happy to finish the job if she returns without me. Do you mind me asking, Naull, where you were coming from? You're not exactly on the road here, and Fairbye isn't a terribly popular destination."

Naull didn't seem as if she was too eager to answer the question, but after a second or two of glancing back and forth between Jozan and Regdar she said, "I live in a . . . a . . . a sort of country house just north of here."

"Your family's estate?" Jozan asked.

"My teacher's," the young woman answered. From the look on her face, Regdar could tell she didn't want to elaborate. Instead she changed the subject. "You three don't look like you come from Fairbye."

"Just passing through," Regdar said.

"On your way to . . . ?" Naull asked.

"We need to clean up this spider problem," answered Jozan, "then Regdar and I are on our way to New Koratia."

Naull's eyes sparkled, and she grinned, showing straight white teeth. "I'm in," she said.

Lidda threw herself to the ground, flopping over on her back. "What is it with you people and these thrice bedamned spiders?"

"Justice, Lidda," Jozan said. "Have you learned nothing?"

Lidda closed her eyes and said, "Is it too late to just be lynched like a normal person?"

They found pieces of a dead raccoon and knew they were on the right track. It was getting dark fast, and Regdar was getting nervous even faster. The spiders were dangerous enough when they were easy to see, but the deeper they got into the forest, the more they walked, the more the deep wound in Regdar's calf reminded him of just how dangerous the creatures could be.

"Webs here," Lidda whispered. There was something about the dark woods that made them all want to whisper.

Regdar looked up and saw that the web went sixty feet or more up the tall, old-growth firs. He had his sword in his hand but couldn't see any spiders.

Something heavy crashed through the underbrush behind him, and he whirled, his sword out in front of him. There was just barely enough light filtering through the tall trees for Regdar to see that it was Naull.

She looked up at him from the ground, pine needles scattered in her hair and clinging to her clothes.

"Sorry," she said. "I tripped."

Naull smiled weakly, and Regdar sheathed his sword. "Let's move away from these webs and camp."

"Camp?" Lidda asked. "You mean sleep out here?"

"It's dark," Regdar said. "We can't even see to walk. It's too dangerous."

Regdar looked at Jozan, who nodded and started moving off into the darkness. Naull stood up and brushed the pine needles and dirt off her clothes.

"Afraid of the dark, Rudlor?" Lidda asked, her head tipped to one side and her voice almost squeaking she was trying so hard to tease him.

He smiled at her and said, "My name is Regdar."

He turned and followed Jozan, not turning around when he heard the two women giggling behind him. Ahead, the trees were beginning to thin out. Jozan was heading for the clearing, exactly as Regdar would have done. The farther they went, the more stars Regdar could see behind the trees, and he started to feel a whole lot better.

They had been going uphill for a long time, and Regdar's leg was throbbing. Jozan was sort of a purple blur ahead of him in the darkness. He came out of the trees into the clearing, and in front of him was a wide swath of pure black darkness. Regdar could make out the rumpled lines and jagged shadows of bare rock above and to the sides of the huge dark space. Jozan stopped walking, and Regdar halted several paces behind him, just out of the line of trees. Naull and Lidda stepped up on either side of the fighter.

"What is that?" Naull asked in hushed tones.

Regdar shook his head.

Jozan said, "Shade your eyes. I'm going to cast a spell."

The priest bent at the waist and picked something up off the ground. Regdar squinted and listened as Jozan murmured a prayer.

After just a few seconds there was a burst of bright light. Regdar closed his eyes and saw spots flash behind his eyelids. He opened his eyes carefully and saw that Jozan was holding the light in his right hand. It wasn't too bright to look at once Regdar's eyes adjusted, but it had the effect of transforming the area around them. The deep shadows filled in, and colors came out of the murk.

"That's handy," Lidda remarked.

"Yeah," said Naull. "I can do that too."

They were standing in front of a tall ridge, an almost vertical wall in front of them where it looked like a huge part of the hillside had split and fallen off—a million years or so before. At the base of the stone wall was the black space Regdar had seen before Jozan cast his light spell. It was the mouth of an immense cave.

Regdar walked up closer to Jozan. The cave mouth opened not only on the face of the cliff but underneath it as well. Jozan's light was bright, but they could barely see a few feet down the hole that emptied into pitch-black nothingness.

Jozan lifted the object he'd picked up off the ground, and Regdar realized that it was a rock—a rock that was glowing with Pelor's light. The two of them walked closer to the edge of the gaping pit, and they could see farther down, maybe ten or fifteen feet. The cave was jagged, natural rock on all sides and deeper than Jozan's light could penetrate. The floor of the shaft sloped down at an angle only a bit more extreme than the hill they'd been climbing through the forest. Regdar figured he could probably keep his footing walking down it.

"Let me guess," Lidda whispered, walking slowly up to join them with Naull in tow. "The spiders came from there."

They all looked at each other, and both Regdar and Jozan shrugged.

"We might assume so," Jozan said, "but let's see."

He lifted the rock and drew back to throw it.

"Wait," Regdar said. The priest stopped. "We could use that light."

"It only lasts ten minutes or so," Naull said, and Jozan glanced back at her. "Am I right?"

"She's right," Jozan said with a smirk.

Jozan hurled the rock into the dark cave. It was a good throw, and the rock arced over the pit then hit the slope and clattered down. All four of them took a step closer and watched the brightly lit rock roll downward, revealing nothing as it went but more uneven rock, scattered with gravel and stones—until it disappeared over an abrupt edge about a hundred and fifty feet down the slope.

Regdar listened carefully and heard the rock hit something, but just barely. He was about to say something when Lidda spoke.

"It's still falling . . . there . . . maybe, what? Ninety feet from the drop-off at the bottom of the slope?"

They all looked at her in the starlight. Regdar couldn't make out her face, then she smiled. and her teeth seemed to glow in the dim purple light.

"Hey," she said, "it's a halfling thing."

Regdar sighed and said, "We'll camp here."

With the drought there was no shortage of dry wood to be found. Regdar made one fire, then set about making six more, forming a circle of smaller campfires around the first one. None of them had encountered spiders like the ones they'd fought earlier, but it seemed a reasonable assumption that the creatures would shy away from fire. Regdar figured that even if the spiders were brave enough to approach the flames, at least the light would help them be seen. Both Naull and Jozan had offered to help him, but he'd gracefully refused. The enterprise gave Regdar something to do, and the idea of a campfire chat with the priest and the two strange women didn't appeal to him. He found Lidda's teasing foolish, and there was something about Naull that was distracting.

"So, Lidda," Naull asked, "how did you end up with Jozan and Regdar? Jozan said something about someone wanting to hang you?"

"The good people of Fairbye," Lidda said, "are a pack of blood-thirsty murderers—and racists too. They kill halflings on sight."

Jozan laughed and said, "And thieves, interestingly enough."

"You're a thief?" Naull asked the halfling.

"I'm an adventurer," Lidda responded.

Regdar almost laughed at that. He looked up long enough to see Naull smile and gaze into the star-spattered sky.

"Adventurer . . ." the young woman said.

"I told the burgher I would question you thoroughly," Jozan said. "If you've stolen something, you should admit your crime and make proper restitution. Stealing the odd this or that shouldn't bring a death sentence, but one can't expect to simply—"

"The burgher is a whoremonger," Lidda said.

There was a space of silence, then Naull asked, "In Fairbye?"

"Sure," Lidda answered. "Fairbye sits on a trade road. Caravans pass through there. Not often, mind you, but they pass through, as do other travelers, like yourselves. Burgher Tomma provides weary travelers with a little . . . well, you know."

"Returning an accusation with an accusation is not a defense, Lidda," Jozan scolded.

"It's true," she said. "My first night there he approached me in the tavern. He put his hand on my thigh and whispered lewd suggestions in my ear."

Naull giggled and asked, "Really? Like what?"

Lidda scuttled closer to the young mage and said, "Well, first of all he told me that if I put his—"

"Ladies," Jozan interrupted, "for the love of Pelor, remember yourselves."

Regdar was happy that no one could see him blush in the darkness.

"Sorry, Father," Naull said.

"Yeah, Pops," Lidda giggled, "my bad."

"You can call me Father," Jozan said, "or Jozan, thank you. You know, it's customary to show some gratitude when people do you a service."

"Is that a sermon?" the halfling asked.

Her petulance was beginning to grate on Regdar, and he felt his jaw clench. Jozan said nothing.

After a few moments, Naull said, "I think what Jozan's trying to say is—"

"I know what he's trying to say," Lidda cut in. "He's right, I guess. Thank you, Jozan, for getting me off the hook, but eventually you'll have to let me go on my way. I pay my debts. You saved me from swinging, and Naull saved me from the spiders, so I'll see this fool's errand through. In the meantime, please don't preach to me. No offense, but you don't know me. You don't know where I come from or what I do or why I—"

She stopped, and Regdar thought she might be crying.

"We should get some sleep," Regdar said, waving his hand over the last fire, which had caught nicely. "I'll take first watch. Naull, please relieve me in a few hours."

Naull was tired, but she hadn't slept. Eventually, she just couldn't pretend anymore and sat up. Regdar barely spoke to her, he just curled up in his bedroll, looking a bit odd without his armor on. He was asleep in seconds.

She tended the fires and scanned the darkness around them for signs of movement. She kept her spells in mind, ready for anything, and was surprised to find that she wasn't the slightest bit afraid. There might be giant spiders out there, or worse, but she was almost deliriously happy. She was out. She was doing it. Like Lidda, she was an adventurer. The word was like medicine to her. *Adventurer*.

She knew the instant she heard the sound of gravel shifting that it was a spider. She looked up and over at where the sound had come from and saw nothing in the firelight. Taking up her staff, she listened for a long time before she heard the sound again. It came from a bit farther away and to the left.

Naull reached down and touched Regdar on the shoulder, then yelped when the huge fighter sat bolt upright. By the time Naull realized Regdar was awake, he had tossed off his bedroll and reached for the shield that he'd been carrying on his back. Naull recognized the spindly red dragon painted on the shield as the sigil of the Duke of Koratia.

"Regdar—" Naull started, but he held out a hand to quiet her.

She heard the sound again, a bit to the right this time, then again almost immediately and from much farther to the left.

Lidda snored loudly and turned over in her sleep. Regdar bent and picked up a short bow. He slung a quiver of arrows over his shoulder just as Jozan sat up, a crossbow already in his hands. Naull was amazed at how well armed these people were. Regdar nocked an arrow and lifted the bow. Jozan did the same, sliding up to his feet. Lidda was still breathing regularly, letting loose the odd dainty snore.

Naull brought a spell to mind that would launch a bolt of magical energy at a spider, one that would never miss its target, but she'd have to be able to see the spider to make it work.

She stood slowly, her hands on her staff but still ready to cast the spell, then something burst out of the darkness. She jumped away as something clattered to the ground next to her. Regdar let loose his arrow, and it streaked out into the darkness. There was a loud scuffling of feet in the shadows, coming from several directions at once.

She looked down and saw that what had come out of the woods was a straight wooden pole about four feet long, carved and burned to a sharp point on one end—a crude javelin.

"It's not the spiders," she said.

Lidda snored again, and Regdar nocked another arrow, scanning the darkness but obviously not seeing anything.

"Are those people out there?" Naull asked, looking at the javelin then at Regdar. "What do we do?"

He didn't answer. Instead, he fired another arrow into the darkness. Naull thought she heard it pass through tree branches.

"Regdar," she whispered. "What do we do?"

He glanced over at her as he nocked another arrow, and a cold chill ran down Naull's spine at the look on his face. He didn't know.

Another javelin came out of the darkness and spanked off Regdar's shield. The big man cursed. Naull realized all at once that they were standing in the middle of a ring of campfires. Whoever—or whatever—was out there could see them.

"Regdar, wait!" she gasped, grabbing his arm just as he began to draw his bow back again. He looked at her and she said, "We can't see them, but they can see us."

She touched the arrow lightly and nodded to him. He opened his mouth but didn't say anything. The look in his eyes was a mixture of curiosity and impatience. He was going to trust her but not for long.

With her staff leaning against her body, she started to chant the words of the spell as she fished in her pouches for the proper material component. She had to look through more than one and had almost completed the incantation when she found the right pouch and pulled out a dead butterfly, pinched between two fingers. The dried insect disappeared almost before she'd gotten it completely out of her pocket, and she spoke the last word of the spell.

The arrow blazed with a bright, almost blinding yellow light, and Naull said, "Shoot it!"

Regdar pulled back the bowstring and let loose. Naull squinted up at him and saw that his eyes were closed. The magically illuminated arrow shot out into the darkness, lighting a patch of the world as it went. Naull saw the trees, the ground, the stones all around in vivid, colorful detail—then there were new sounds.

Something grunted, growled, there was a sound that might have been a yelp, and Naull saw a shadow running through the trees. It was just the black outline of a person, a little person no taller than Lidda but more stoutly built. It was running from the light.

The arrow landed in the underbrush, and they all watched, listening, for the ten minutes it took for the light to flicker, then go out. There were no more footsteps and no more javelins.

Lidda yawned, and Naull looked over and saw the halfling sit up slowly. She looked around, squinting, and asked, "What . . . my turn to be the lookout or something?"

Everyone stared at her.

Lidda looked back at them and said, "What?"

"**Small humanoids**," Regdar said, standing slowly from where he'd been crouching and examining the ground. "Goblins, maybe ... or halflings."

Lidda snored loudly, a response that elicited a giggle from Naull and a scowl from Jozan. Regdar blushed, glancing at Naull as Jozan began to stalk back to the campsite, no doubt to rouse the halfling, who had been sleeping for at least an hour after the others had risen with the dawn. As Jozan passed Regdar, he stopped, looking down.

"Regdar," the priest said, "are you wounded?"

The big fighter looked down at his boot. It was crusted with blood that had been drying around the makeshift bandage he'd tied while the others slept.

"It's fine," he said.

Jozan sighed impatiently and squatted next to Regdar. "Was this a spider that bit you?" he asked. Not waiting for an answer, the priest added, "Take your boot off."

Regdar opened his mouth to tell the priest again that he was fine but ended up taking off his boot.

"For Pelor's sake, Regdar. . . ." Jozan grumbled.

"Those spiders could be poisonous," Naull said, squinting at the wound from over Jozan's shoulder.

Regdar felt foolish and avoided looking at Naull.

"She's right," Jozan said, poking at the wound with one finger. "Still, I don't see any sign of poisoning or infection."

"Very well, then," Regdar said. "I'm fine, and we haven't even begun to explore the—"

He stopped when a rush of warmth enveloped his leg and the throbbing pain that he'd grown accustomed to was suddenly gone. Jozan was kneeling, with his head bowed, whispering something Regdar couldn't hear. A dim golden light radiated from his hands, then faded just as Regdar realized what was happening. Jozan had called upon the power of Pelor to heal him.

The priest stood, nodded once at Regdar, then walked back toward their campsite. Naull was still looking at his leg.

"How does it feel?" she asked.

"Fine," Regdar answered. He looked down at his leg and saw not the slightest trace of a wound.

The captured goblins stood in the center of the deep pit, keeping close together. Tzrg sat squeezed together with a line of his fellow Stonedeep goblins. Rezrex and his hobgoblins sat on the higher ledge above them, swilling the bitter fungus beer and laughing heartily at the goblins in the pit.

Tzrg wasn't laughing. He knew what was going to happen to the captured goblins. They had done terrible things to the Cavemouth Tribe at Rezrex's command, and things were just getting worse.

Rezrex growled, "*Brjdn ksr!*"

Tzrg cringed and wanted to close his eyes but didn't. He heard stone grind on stone and instinctively looked down. He sat on a ledge five feet below the floor level. Another fifteen feet below that ledge was the floor of the pit. Almost directly under where Tzrg was sitting was the entrance to a little side passage that emptied out onto the uneven floor of the pit. It was from this side passage that the grinding noise, then the monster, came.

The two captured goblins saw it right away, and though they were scared at first, Tzrg could see them force themselves to face the creature. They looked at it as if they didn't know what it was, which didn't surprise Tzrg. He'd only seen two of them himself.

The Cavemouth goblins were unarmed, which wasn't fair. They bent their knees as if waiting to jump at the *ksr*, and clenched their fists, then opened their hands again and bent their fingers into claws. They bared their fangs and growled at the beast.

The creature stepped forward slowly, its powerful muscles sublimely evident under its thin, shimmering coat of gray-and-brown mottled fur. It was big but not enormous. It was a little longer than a goblin was tall, with a bushy tail as long as its body. The creature's tail whipped around behind it as it advanced. A shaggy mane of dark gray fur ruffled up over its shoulders, bristling as it hunched down, stalking forward.

A cheer went up from the hobgoblins that was mimicked by the bulk of the Stonedeep goblins. Tzrg cheered with them, if reluctantly, and hoped it would be over soon, so he could find some dark corner of the cave and just get drunk or something. The *ksr* growled at the crowd, and that scared most of the goblins into silence. The distraction also gave the two Cavemouth goblins time to whisper to each other and flash a couple quick signs. They split up, trying to circle the beast, so that it could only see one of them at a time. Tzrg was impressed by how smart that was. These were smart goblins. They might live as long as two or three minutes.

One of the goblins was stepping back away from the creature while the other was moving just a little closer. They both continued to separate. They were scanning the floor of the pit, presumably for loose stones or anything they might use as a weapon. All the stalagmites had been broken off and carted away a long time before, and Rezrex had the whole thing swept out before every "fight." That's what Rezrex liked to call this: *pnl* . . . a fight. Tzrg had helped sweep the pit out himself and hadn't dared leave anything in there for the Cavemouth goblins. Their fate was sealed.

The monster looked from one goblin to the other before seeming to decide on one—the smaller of the two. It lunged forward, and the smaller goblin jumped back, losing his balance and falling on his seat. The goblin scrambled backward, apparently not realizing that the creature had stopped. The second goblin leaped at the *ksr* and was committed to the attack before he realized the thing wasn't still going after his friend.

The monster turned on the attacking goblin, and Tzrg winced at what happened next. The fur, even the skin, peeled back from the *ksr*'s face, revealing glistening pink muscle and shining yellow-white bone. It's fang-studded jaws came open, and it let out a shrieking wail that rattled Tzrg's eardrums. He put his hands to his ears—as did the rest of the Stonedeep goblins—but he could still hear the scream. He couldn't hear Rezrex's shout of triumph and excitement, though, so that was one good thing. The huge hobgoblin was having the time of his life.

The goblin who had begun a gutsy assault on the much larger and fiercer *ksr* scrambled to a halt and ended up falling on the cave floor in front of the monster, arms and legs sprawled out and his face twisted into a very un-goblinlike expression of pure horror.

The goblin looked as if he wanted to get away, but he couldn't. He wasn't frozen or paralyzed so much as confused with pure, unadulterated terror. The creature pounced, and the goblin wasn't able to do much but shake and sob as the monster ripped it to bloody shreds.

Rezrex leaped to his feet, cheering, looking more pleased with himself than he was with his pet *ksr*. Tzrg looked down at the smaller Cavemouth goblin, who was trying in vain to climb the smooth flowstone walls of the *ksr* pit as the creature, blood dripping from its baggy-skinned jaws, advanced on him slowly to the cheers of the hobgoblins and goblins that echoed around the massive chamber.

Tzrg turned away, sure that eventually he would share the Cavemouth goblins' fate.

Regdar stood next to Naull at the edge of the deep black shaft. Jozan stood on the other side of Naull, and Regdar could hear Lidda getting dressed behind them.

He looked down into the shaft and watched as four balls of what looked like torchlight gradually sank through the air, slowly turning around each other, twisting and intertwining, and all the way illuminating the irregular walls of the vertical cave.

"How deep did you say they'll go?" Regdar asked Naull.

She didn't look at him, just kept her eyes glued to the descending lights. "They'll go out when they're a hundred and ten feet away from me," she whispered, her voice a flat monotone.

Jozan sighed and scratched at the stubble on his chin. They watched until the lights finally revealed what looked like a floor.

"Ninety feet," Naull said.

From where they were standing it was difficult to see much detail at the bottom of the great pit, but Regdar thought there might have been at least one side passage. The floor had a steep downward slope, reversing itself in a zigzag shape that turned the shaft back under them.

Naull's magical lights flickered once then went out, leaving the cave once more a wide void of impenetrable blackness.

"That hundred and ten feet seems unusually precise," Jozan said. "When you stunned the spiders yesterday you told us your magic was not an exact science, now it seems that it is."

Naull rubbed her eyes and replied, "I've been working with a teacher. We've measured this spell. The effects of the spell I cast on the spiders can vary depending on what it's cast on, and I've never seen those spiders before, but the dancing lights are always the same. I was moving them at a regular pace and counting."

"I did see a bottom," Jozan said. "Regdar?"

Regdar exhaled slowly through his nose and took a step closer to the edge. He kicked a little stone off the edge, and that must have startled Naull. She gasped and put a hand lightly on his armored elbow. He turned to her, and she snatched her hand away.

"Be careful," she said, turning away from him.

Regdar stood still as she moved away, then said to Jozan, "I'm not sure, but it did look like we could at least rest there."

"Rest where?" Lidda asked from behind him.

Regdar turned, looked down at her, then turned back to the pit. Lidda laughed.

Jozan said, "He's quite serious, Lidda."

The halfling stopped laughing. "I'm not sure I can approve that plan," she said.

Before Jozan could chastise her, Naull said, "Frankly, my friends, I'm not sure I can either. I mean . . . I don't think I could climb down there. I mean . . ."

"I can," Regdar said.

Jozan looked down into the darkness and scratched at his chin again. "I have to admit," he said, his quiet voice still echoing in the wide cave mouth, "I'm not much of a climber myself."

"Are there spiders down there?" Lidda asked, rubbing eyes still puffy from her long night's sleep.

"We tracked them here," Jozan answered.

"But it wasn't spiders that attacked us last night," said Naull.

Regdar looked back at their campsite and let his eyes roam slowly over their various packs and pouches. He didn't see any rope at all, much less a hundred feet or more of it. It would be a free-climb, something more like what a thief might learn how to do.

"Lidda can make the climb," Regdar said. "Can't you, Lidda."

The halfling stopped rubbing her face and looked up at the big fighter. There was something about the look on her face that made Regdar unsure whether she was about to laugh or attack him.

"I don't like the idea of splitting up," Jozan said.

Regdar nodded to Jozan, but quickly turned back to Lidda. "Well?" he asked.

"Sure," she said, peering down at the huge hole, surely unable to fathom its depths from where she was standing, "I can make any climb you can make, Redbar, but Naull and the good father can't. So, what say we head for New Koratia . . . or maybe Zarreth?"

Regdar turned back to the cave and said to Jozan, "Lidda will go down first, picking out the easiest climb as she goes. She'll let you and Naull know how to follow. I'll go last. If we can rig up something—anything like a rope, I could tie it between myself and—"

"Or," Lidda said, "Regular here can climb my—"

"Lidda," Jozan interrupted.

The halfling threw up her hands and turned back to the campsite but didn't walk away. Regdar watched her, a hand over his mouth made him, he hoped, look thoughtful. He was really trying to silence a laugh. Lidda reminded him of his days in the duke's infantry. She was ribbing him like soldiers do, and she was good at it.

Lidda put one arm behind her back, grabbed that wrist with her other hand, and started to stretch as if in preparation for a climb.

Regdar was happy to find that the shaft wall wasn't as steep as it looked from above. Though hardly an easy climb—no climb was easy wearing scale mail and a good thirty pounds of weapons and gear—he knew he'd get them all down safely. Looking down he saw Naull just below him. He was most worried about her. She seemed more afraid than he'd assumed she'd be. She'd faced down the spiders easily enough, but something about either the height they were climbing from (or, more accurately, the depth they were climbing into) or the darkness that constantly nibbled at the edges of the light from Lidda's lantern was causing her hands to shake. She was pale and ghostly even backlit from Lidda's lantern, and she often gasped and made other uncertain noises.

Regdar hadn't hoped on being quiet by any stretch of the imagination, but there was a crucial difference between the sound of the approach of a heavily armed, heavily armored, confident party, and the descent of a confused group of nervous women. Regdar had no doubt that something—spider, humanoid, or worse—was waiting for them at the bottom of the shaft. He only hoped that they would have any advantage left against it when it made itself known.

Jozan was nearly as nervous about the climb, and nearly as taxed by it, as Naull. He didn't complain—Jozan seemed incapable of that—but his shield kept bumping into his crossbow, which bumped into his mace, which bumped into his armor over and over again all the way down. The noises reminded Regdar of a one-man-band he'd seen perform in the marketplace in New Koratia.

For her part, Lidda was a marvel. She climbed with the grace of a monkey, the lantern dangling from her belt hardly swinging at all. She was obviously holding back, keeping close enough to them so that they could all benefit from her light. Between Jozan's cacophony, Naull's grunted curses, and the creak of his own armor, Regdar couldn't hear her move at all. She was also smart enough to refrain from speaking—to Regdar's mind a small miracle—and he was sure the little halfling was enjoying herself.

Regdar couldn't help but think that the lengths they were going to to defend a village's sheep herds might have been a bit extreme. Though he wasn't in the habit of questioning priests of Pelor, Regdar wasn't so sure that Jozan was thinking only of Fairbye's herds. They had been traveling together for only a little while, but Regdar got the feeling that Jozan was in no particular hurry to return to the city. The farther they'd traveled from the Duchy of Koratia's eastern frontier, the more Jozan seemed to want to slow their progress.

Regdar pushed these idle thoughts from his mind when he heard a sharp hiss below him. Lidda was clinging to the wall with one hand and holding her lantern up by its belt strap. She caught his eye and turned her head sharply to her left. When Regdar followed her gaze he saw something glowing faintly at the edge of the lantern's light.

It was a line of some kind, hanging down along the wall of the shaft. If it was rope, it was made of some kind of bleached hemp or other material Regdar had never seen before. It disappeared into shadows above and below so he couldn't tell how high up the shaft it was tied or how deep it hung.

Regdar nodded at the halfling. She let her lantern hang from her belt once more, and started scrambling sideways along the rough wall, moving smoothly but cautiously toward the line. Jozan and Naull had both noticed the exchange and had stopped climbing. They hung close to the wall, panting, both obviously happy for the chance to rest but feeling only less secure clinging to the wall when something might be hanging there with them.

Lidda stopped once to peer at the mysterious line from a closer vantage point, then Regdar watched her scramble the rest of the way to it. She reached out and took hold of the line, testing its weight a little.

She looked up at Regdar and whispered something, but he couldn't quite make it out. He had two good footholds and a decent handhold, so he let go with one hand, held it to his ear, and widened his eyes at her. Even from so far below him, he could see that she was irritated at his inability to hear, and that embarrassed him a bit.

She let go of the line and climbed up toward him. Regdar was impressed by how quickly she was no more than arm's length from him.

"What are you, deaf?" she whispered. "It's a rope ladder."

Regdar narrowed his eyes and peered at the line again, still not able to make out any detail. He looked down at the others and with a hoarse voice whispered, "It's a rope ladder. Climb over to it."

"It doesn't look very big," Lidda told him. "I doubt it'll hold all four of us."

"Let Naull and Jozan take it, then," Regdar said. "We're better climbers."

Lidda looked like she was about to make some kind of nasty remark, but she didn't. Instead, she said, "I'll help Naull."

The halfling scurried down and across to Naull, and Regdar could hear her whispering encouragement and advice to the shaking, uncertain young mage. Jozan began his clanging, clumsy way toward the ladder himself.

Soon enough, they were all gathered around the strange rope ladder, clinging to the craggy walls like so many giant bugs—an image Regdar wasn't altogether comfortable with, given the fact that for all they knew the cave was crawling with spiders.

"Will it . . . hold . . . us?" Naull asked Lidda, her whispered words coming out between great gulps of air.

Lidda tugged on the rope. It hummed quietly but held fast.

The halfling pulled it toward the young woman and said, "There's only one way to find out."

Naull nodded and reached out for the rope.

"Wait," Regdar said. He took hold of one of Naull's shoulder straps, his hand closing tightly over an empty pouch. She looked up at him and smiled weakly. "All right," he said.

Naull reached out and grabbed one rung of the ladder.

"It's sticky," she said, looking at Lidda.

The halfling shrugged and said, "I'm not sure what it's made out of, but it's not too much stickier than mead spilled on a table. You'll be able to let go."

Regdar examined the rope closely and was confounded by it. It wasn't braided like normal rope. It almost looked like each line, as big around as Regdar's thumb, was made from a single solid strand of something more like silk than any plant fiber. The two sides of the ladder were spaced close together—so close Regdar wasn't sure he'd be able to get even one of his heavy boots onto a rung, let alone both. The steps of the ladder were spaced closer together than they needed to be, and to Regdar the thing looked like a child's toy.

Naull set one foot on a ladder rung and glanced up at Regdar. He smiled, holding her tightly, and she stepped away from the wall. The ladder only swung a little bit, and Regdar was able to not only hold onto Naull but steady her on the ladder as well. The young woman cursed under her breath and closed her eyes, waiting for the ladder to stop swaying. Regdar kept his hand tight around the pouch but gradually let her weight fall on the ladder.

"It's holding her," Lidda said.

Regdar let all of Naull's weight fall on the ladder, and after a few moments while the others stared at him expectantly, he let go of Naull's pouch. When his hand came away, Naull sighed and opened her eyes.

"I think it's all right," she said. "It's sticky, but it's holding me."

Jozan, who was a little bit farther down the wall than Naull, took hold of the ladder. It swayed a little and he said, "Hold on."

Naull held her breath while the priest climbed onto the ladder. Regdar held his hand half an inch from Naull's shoulder, ready to grab her should the ladder give way. The lines swayed a bit more but held fast.

"I think this is spider silk," Jozan said.

Naull let out a hissing breath and said, "Don't say that. Even if it's true."

Jozan started climbing down.

Regdar and Lidda exchanged a look as Naull started to slowly follow the priest down the spidersilk ladder.

"I'd rather stick to the wall," Lidda said with a wink.

"It was left to burn itself out," Lidda said, crouching next to a blackened fire pit at the bottom of the shaft. "It's been cold for days . . . maybe weeks."

Regdar nodded and looked over at Jozan, who was just stepping off the spidersilk ladder onto the sloping cave floor at the bottom of the shaft. Naull was following him, descending faster, having grown more comfortable with the ladder. The fighter turned his attention to the floor of the dark cave, lit by Lidda's lantern.

Scattered all about were bits of refuse, most of which Regdar couldn't immediately identify. He reached down and picked up a set of crude tongs. The tool was as long as his arm and fashioned from some sort of hooklike . . . somethings . . . tied with spidersilk to the end of two thick sticks. The hooks almost looked like bones but felt more like fingernails.

Jozan moved up next to him and said, "I think they're called 'pedipalps.' "

Regdar turned and gave him a confused look.

"Spider teeth," the priest explained with a wink.

Regdar set the tool down carefully on the cave floor, half tempted to compare the sharp hooks with the wound in his leg— but the wound was gone.

Naull stepped off the ladder and began wiping her hands on her cloak with a disgusted sneer.

"Well," Lidda said, standing, her hands on her narrow hips, "the gang's all here. What now, Daddy?"

Jozan raised an eyebrow and said, "Now, my child, we . . ."

The priest was obviously annoyed at not being properly addressed, but more than that Regdar realized Jozan wasn't sure what they should do next.

"What kind of bowl is this?" Naull asked from the shadows near the cave wall, her voice echoing in barely audible pings all around them.

She was holding a wide, shallow bowl of some beige material that might have been porcelain. When she turned it over and saw the brown **X** emblazoned across it, she shrieked, stepped back, and flung the thing away from her. The spider carapace clattered along the floor, bouncing but not breaking.

The sound echoed all around and almost masked Jozan's quiet voice. "They use them to make tools," the priest said.

"What?" Naull asked.

"The spiders," Lidda answered for him. "Whoever lives down here kills the spiders, maybe eats them, then uses the shells to make tools. Kobolds?"

Regdar took in the scene: fire, crude tools with only rudimentary craftsmanship, no sign of metal. The cave was obviously home to some primitive race, and by the size of the ladder and the shadows that had attacked them from the darkness the night before, they were one of the smaller humanoid races. The ground under a human's feet was home to any number of dangerous primitives. The fact that most of them were afraid of light kept them safely underground where they belonged, but some of them came out, and when they did, it usually meant war. Regdar had battled orcs himself, and gnolls once.

"Kobolds? Maybe," Regdar said. "Could be goblins. Lots of different—"

Lidda stepped forward and shushed him, holding up one tiny, thin-fingered hand. She was looking down the slope of the passage, where the cave emptied into another shaft that they hadn't yet had a chance to examine. Regdar drew his greatsword, and the scream of steel-on-steel as it came out of his scabbard echoed loudly in the confines of the cave.

Lidda lurched at him, eyes wide, teeth clenched together, one finger in front of her scowling lips, shushing him again, silently.

Regdar blushed but didn't say anything. He listened but could hear nothing.

When a crude javelin spanked off the cave floor a inch from Lidda's left foot, the halfling launched herself into the air.

Regdar reached, quickly, sliding the shield off his back and into his left hand with a single lightning-fast, fluid motion. He saw a pair of eyes glowing in the darkness and lifted one foot to step forward—

—and Lidda smashed onto his shield. Momentarily off-balance from the weight of the halfling who, Regdar was dumbfounded to realize, was clinging to his shield with both hands, he stumbled and almost fell. Lidda's legs were tucked up to her chin, her knees and shins pressed hard against the shield.

Another javelin whizzed past Regdar's head. He couldn't turn to watch its path but heard Naull curse loudly. There was a clattering of rocks and scrambling footsteps both behind him and in the shadows ahead. Something leaped from the shadows and Regdar brought his shield up to meet the attack before he realized that Lidda was still hanging there. The creature drew up short, though, hefting another of the primitive javelins—pointed sticks really—for a shorter, easier throw.

Regdar could see in the little humanoid's eyes that it meant to throw the javelin at Lidda, so he stepped toward the attack and threw the shield—and the halfling along with it—off to his left. He saw Lidda's legs and arms spiral past the edge of his peripheral vision and stepped in at the little savage with deadly purpose.

The javelin skipped off the clean edge of Regdar's left pauldron, nearly slicing his stern chin as it passed. He heard Lidda—or was it Naull?—scream in anger, and Jozan was practically shouting what must have been a prayer to Pelor. In that same instant, Regdar sliced up with his greatsword, the tip of the blade tracing an arc from Regdar's left ankle to well above his head and almost straight out to his right. In the middle, the heavy blade passed cleanly through the little humanoid's midsection, cutting it open and spilling its guts on the cave floor.

"Goblins!" Lidda called out from behind him.

Regdar set his jaw and stepped in as he saw another one emerging from the shadows along the opposite cave wall. This one held a club carved from a stout branch and studded with sharpened stones. Regdar hacked his sword down in front of him and moved to pierce the goblin's chest when the cave went white, and pain forced his eyes closed.

He heard something—likely the goblin in front of him—scream with pain. Someone bumped into him from behind. He whirled, his eyes refusing to open as purple blotches bubbled across the inside of his eyelids.

"Damn it, Jozan," he heard Naull say from behind him—it must have been she who'd bumped him, "warn us when you're going to cast—"

Regdar tried to step away from her, but she tripped or was pushed into the back of his knees. He tensed his legs, but he still went down. Regdar opened his eyes and had to shut them again. He hadn't realized how accustomed to the darkness his eyes had become. Naull cursed again when Regdar hit the cave floor, rolling over his left arm and bumping her a few times as he tried to roll to his feet.

"Regdar," Naull yelled, "look out for the—"

Again she was cut off by Regdar falling. He was rolling and sliding down a hard rock incline, and from the sound of her cursing and growling, Naull was close behind. He opened his eyes, and the light was gone, replaced by a darkness so total, Regdar was sure he was blind. He hit a rock wall, and the air was forced from his lungs, but he bounced off and continued to fall. He felt Naull grab his arm, but the hand was forced away before he could reach her.

He could hear Jozan call his name, but the sound of the priest's voice was receding quickly, echoing, and impossible to pin down. In a heartbeat or two it was gone completely.

What a bunch of amateurs, he thought. What a bunch of damned amateurs we are.

8

So they're goblins then, Jozan thought as he stepped into the shadowy humanoid's charge.

Lidda was sprawled out on the cave floor next to him, cursing in some language Jozan didn't recognize, all tangled up with Regdar's shield. From behind the priest came loud crashing sounds, rocks and gravel shifting, and the curses of both Regdar and Naull. With the light from Lidda's lantern partially blocked by the big shield on top of her, Jozan had enough trouble seeing the goblin that was attacking him. He had no idea what his friends were doing.

A second goblin, the one Jozan had cast the light spell on, had disappeared down a side passage, the bright light going with him. The spell had blinded the creature but had also managed to do much the same to all of them, and Jozan was more than a little embarrassed by that failure.

The goblin jabbed at Jozan, the roughly carved tip of the little javelin looking sharp enough to kill. The priest batted the stick away with his heavy steel mace, and the weapon flew from the goblin's grip. With a squeal, the little humanoid turned and ran. Jozan, his mace still on the follow-through, stepped back and let his weapon fall in front of him in a defensive posture. The goblin was running a—

It fell with a weak, high-pitched scream when a thin-handled dagger appeared as if from thin air, stuck in the middle of its back. The goblin went down hard, never putting its hands out to stop its fall.

"Bull's-eye!" Lidda cheered.

The priest looked down at her in horror. The creature was running away, and she'd hit it in the back. The lack of honor, the absence of a sense of justice, made Jozan's blood run cold.

Before he could speak, the halfling was up and running in the direction the fleeing goblin had gone, the light of her lantern going with her. Jozan reached down and snatched up Regdar's heavy shield before it became too dark for him to see it.

"Lidda!" the priest shouted as he started to run after her.

She hared off after the fleeing, light-blinded goblin, into the black depths of the side passage from which the three goblins had emerged, away from wherever Regdar and Naull had gone.

The cave floor was almost impossible for Jozan to negotiate. He could see the light from Lidda's lantern, bouncing and blinking as she, apparently, dodged between the stalagmites that crowded the floor. Jozan bumped his knees and other parts of his anatomy on more than a few of the conical stones that grew from the cave floor like tree stumps.

He had only prayed for the one light spell that morning and was further embarrassed by the fact that he carried no torches or lantern of his own. If he lost sight of Lidda's bobbing light, he would be at Pelor's mercy in the dead black cave all alone.

There was a sound from ahead—at least Jozan thought it was ahead of him, the sound echoing a thousand times over made that a wild guess at best. Lidda's lantern seemed to bobble in response to it. It sounded like someone being strangled, and Jozan feared for the halfling's life. She might have run headlong into an ambush. It would be the most obvious tactic: appear to be running away so your enemy follows, cocky and careless, into a nest of archers.

Jozan, unsure what else to do, hefted his mace and went after her as best he could through the stalagmites. The lantern light was no longer moving away, and as the priest came closer, he slowed down, trying as hard as he could not to make a noise. He breathed through his mouth—quieter than breathing through his nose. He walked with a stiff-legged gate to minimize the creaking of his armor, and he held his mace high, so it wouldn't knock against any of the stalagmites.

Finally, he could see Lidda, lit by her own lantern. She was scanning the darkness in his direction and smiled when she saw him.

"It's all right," she called, her voice cascading around the cave.

Jozan looked around and realized that he could see nothing at all outside the strict boundaries of the lamplight. The cave could be barely bigger than that, or stretch on for thousands of feet in all directions. The air was cool and humid, with a distinct breeze that carried on it a melange of dank, earthy smells, one stronger than the others: the smell of blood.

Jozan approached more quickly, his jaw clenched tightly, wondering what he would say to the wayward halfling that might impress upon her his outrage at the way she'd dispatched the fleeing goblin—no, two fleeing goblins.

The light-blinded goblin was impaled on a stalagmite, the surprisingly sharp point of the formation jutting out through its blood-drenched back. Its eyes were closed, but Jozan could see a line of light, and a vein-traced orange glow through its eyelids. He had cast the spell on the goblin's eyes—another old trick.

Jozan looked at Lidda, and she must have seen the stern look on his face.

"It wasn't me," she said. "He just ran into it, poor bugger."

When he'd been a raw recruit in the Duke of Koratia's infantry—The Third New Koratia Comitatus, Red Dragon Regiment, to be precise—the drill sergeant had made the whole regiment perform various tasks while blindfolded. As Regdar fished around through the contents of his backpack, he wished he'd paid better attention to those drills.

"I think I found a torch," Naull said, her voice quiet but still echoing in the absolute darkness, "but I can't find my flint and steel."

The only other sound was the distinct splashing of water, as if from a waterfall, or even waves crashing in rapid succession over stone. Echoes made it impossible to judge distance or direction. Regdar thought they might be either inches from the edge or a mile from it.

Every time his fingers touched something familiar in his backpack, they'd find something that seemed wholly alien in turn. Finally, his hand came to rest on what he was certain was his own flint and steel.

"Thank Pelor," he said, "I think I found mine."

Good," said Naull, "light my torch."

Regdar carefully opened the little suede pouch that held his flint and steel, realizing that if he were to drop it in his haste, he might never find it. All the while, he kept his eyes closed—he remembered somewhere that he was supposed to do that. The purple blotches brought on by the wayward light spell were gone, leaving only the odd flash and trace of red he saw whenever he closed his eyes.

"Do you have it?" Naull asked, impatience making her voice shake.

Regdar felt the cool of the steel and the roughness of the flint and took a deep breath, holding them away from his face—and stopped.

"Regdar?" Naull asked, obviously sensing his hesitation.

"I can't see your torch," he said.

Naull answered with an irritated sigh.

Regdar held the flint and steel carefully in his left hand and pushed his right hand into his backpack again.

"I'll have to find one of mine," he said.

There was a rustling of fabric from the same general direction that Naull's voice had come from, and she said, "I'll try to find my flint and thrice-bedamned steel."

Regdar, irritated himself and amazed at how cavernous his backpack felt now that he couldn't see what was in it, nodded, not realizing that Naull couldn't see the gesture. When his hand finally closed around the rag-covered head of a torch, he sighed and slid it out.

"I have one," he whispered to Naull.

He tapped the flint and steel together and a tiny spark flew, not even shedding enough light for Regdar to see his own fingertips for the slightest second.

"Light it," she urged.

Regdar bit back a response. What did she think he was trying to do? The second spark was bigger, and it leaped from the flint to the ragged edge of the torch cloth. A line of orange glowed in the total darkness and Regdar thought he'd never been happier to see so minute a fire.

"Did it catch?" Naull asked, apparently unable to see the growing line of orange light trace its way along the edge of the rag.

Regdar didn't bother to answer. He puffed air into his cheeks and blew gently. Specks of light jumped from the edges of the rag, then a fire licked up, smaller than a candle flame.

"You got it!" Naull exclaimed, her words pinging through the darkness around them.

In no time, the torch was ablaze, and Regdar turned to survey the place their long fall had brought them to.

They were, as he'd expected, in a natural cave. The chamber was roughly circular, maybe ten yards across. The floor sloped gradually in one direction—Regdar had no way of knowing which way was north, south, east, or west. He didn't even know into which end of the chamber they'd fallen, though he assumed the higher end.

The ceiling was beyond the reach of his torch, though when he held it high over his head, he could see the blunt tips of hundreds of thin stalactites. What dominated the cave, though, and explained the sounds of water, was a thin waterfall that stretched up into darkness and emptied into a pool of roughly churning water.

He looked at Naull, who was also surveying their surroundings. She was a bit haggard, her clothes in a general state of disarray, but as beautiful as—

Regdar pushed that unbidden thought aside and took a few steps closer to the water, looking away from the young mage.

"What do we do?" she asked.

He could feel her looking at him and could feel his face flush. He didn't turn around, just took a couple steps closer to the edge of the pool. There was something about the way the water moved that seemed strange, but he couldn't put his finger on it.

Naull stepped closer to him, and he thought she almost touched his arm, but when he looked down, he saw her pull her hand away.

"That's not just the waterfall," she all but whispered.

"I thought so," Regdar said. "It's kind of . . ."

"Swirling?" she offered, stepping even closer to the edge.

Regdar looked down. They were standing on a flat slab of some kind of smooth white rock. The water wasn't splashing onto it, though, it seemed to . . . swirl . . . under it.

Regdar noticed another sound intruding on the splash of the water, and just as he opened his mouth to warn Naull that the stone was cracking, the slab fell out from under his feet, plunging them both into the icy clutches of the strange little maelstrom.

"I'm not used to working with a partner, all right?" Lidda finally admitted.

They were picking their way back through the dark forest of stalagmites, and with every step, Jozan grew less and less sure that they would ever find the bottom of the shaft, let alone Regdar and Naull. Though he knew he was taking some of his nervousness and frustration out on the halfling, it didn't change the fact that they were in this predicament because of Lidda's irresponsible actions. He was peering into the utter blackness all around them, hoping to see anything, so he didn't respond to Lidda's halfhearted admission.

"Now I get the silent treatment," she grumbled. "Priests . . ."

Jozan wasn't listening. He was angry with her, but anger was a fleeting thing, unworthy of Pelor's servants. He could feel that Lidda had a good heart and was confident that she could be turned around. It was that feeling for people that led him to the service of Pelor, that same empathy that got him in so much trouble in the past.

Lidda stayed close to him, the light from her lantern the only hope they had to avoid the fate of the impaled goblin let alone find their way back. Jozan tried to keep his attention to the outer perimeter of the light so that he could see whatever there was to see as soon as it was possible for him to see it. Even so, he knew he'd only have a second or two to react. When he saw the web, he reached out to grab Lidda's arm but misjudged the distance between them and almost pushed her over.

"For Olidammara's sake, Jozan," she spat, more surprised than angry. "I said I was sorry, what do you want me to do—"

Jozan shushed her and pointed at the web while slipping his mace off the ring on his belt. He heard Lidda draw her sword.

"We went the wrong way," she whispered.

Jozan started moving slowly toward he web and was about to shush her again when a long, low moan echoed through the pitch-black cave. It was the unmistakable sound of someone in pain. Jozan could feel it. The hair on the backs of his arms stood on end. The voice had the sound of someone who had given up hope. Jozan had only heard that sound once before, and he'd hoped he'd never hear it again.

"It's Regdar," Lidda said, hopping once, then tearing away at a run.

Jozan reached out to try to stop her, but she slipped past him and was hopping over stalagmites on her way toward a sound that Jozan knew couldn't possibly be Regdar. The priest had no choice but to follow her.

As before, she opened the distance between them quickly. She didn't appear to be slowed by the dense stalagmites. Instead, she seemed to use them to her advantage, leapfrogging some, spinning around others, so that they seemed to be pushing her through the darkness. Jozan followed her as quickly as he could, bumping his knees and elbows, all clanking armor and panting breaths.

There was a loud hiss and everything went black, but that was the least of Regdar's worries. He could feel himself being pulled underwater even as he was whipped to the side. His nose filled with water, and his eyes burned. He clamped his mouth shut and struggled to hold his breath while the fast-moving water had its way with him. His sword was ripped from his hand, and he hit rock—maybe a rock wall—and he was falling.

He could feel his face come out into air, and he drew in a quick gasp, managing to clamp his mouth shut again when water splashed into his face. He bounced off something hard—another rock—and it hurt, but he knew nothing was broken. The air was forced out of his lungs, though, and it was painful, desperate seconds before he came out of the water again long enough to draw in a breath.

There was a splash that whipped his head to one side, and the sound might have been loud enough to deafen him, if his ears hadn't filled with water. He was submerged and sinking, but he wasn't being beaten against rocks anymore. Regdar could feel the water shove him down and backward, then he came to rest on the bottom.

Wrapped in thirty pounds or more of steel armor, he sank like a stone wrapped in thirty pounds or more of steel armor. His feet were on the bottom, a hard stone surface that Regdar was happy to note was less slippery than he'd expect the bottom of a pond to be. He opened his eyes in the frigid water but could see nothing at all. He pushed against the bottom with both feet, confident that he could at least get his face above water long enough to breathe, maybe even to call out for Naull.

The top of his head hit stone only a foot or less above him, and he might have knocked himself out but for the sturdy helm he still wore. The strap around his chin had secured it through what Regdar realized was worse than a one-way trip down a waterfall. The stone above his head kept him submerged, though. His lungs were beginning to ache. He tried again, holding his hands up above him, but felt the smooth stone before he even bothered trying to kick off the floor again. He was completely blind, and he was drowning.

It took Jozan a few moments to realize that the webs were full of goblins. The fine, sticky strands stretched from stalactite to stalagmite and to one uneven, curved wall of the huge cave up into the darkness past the reach of Lidda's lantern light. Studded throughout the chaotic mass of grayish white webbing were bundles of almost pure white, shaped in the outline of the squat little humanoids. Some seemed to be missing limbs, a few were missing heads. Others were hanging upside down or at odd angles. Most were packed into the web in uncomfortable, even unnatural positions, with arms forced at odd angles, legs broken and smashed up against backs.

Lidda stopped at the edge of the mass of webs and, gazing along its length, stepped backward until her back came to rest on Jozan's thigh.

"Let's go," she whispered, her voice echoing in the cool air that was growing ever closer with a strong stench of decay. "Let's just—"

The priest put a hand on her shoulder, and she stopped speaking.

They stood there looking at the webs for the space of a few heartbeats, then Jozan said, "They're all dead. None of them are moving."

"Thank the Nurturing Matriarch for that, at least," Lidda said.

Jozan offered similar thanks, silently, to Pelor, then said, "This could be Fairbye in a week . . . a month . . . maybe a year, if these spiders—"

"Then we won't go back to Fairbye," Lidda cut in. "What are we talking about this for, Jozan? There must be dozens of goblins stuck in there. There could be hundreds, maybe thousands of those spiders or more."

Jozan's heart sank. As always, at least to Jozan's mind, the right thing to do was evident. They needed to continue. They needed to eradicate these spiders before they ranged any farther on the surface, before they established a pantry like this in the village.

But Lidda was right. There would have to be more of the spiders than the two of them could possibly kill. Regdar and Naull were gone—who knew where. They might be dead, at the bottom of a deep shaft if they were lucky, in a web like the goblins if they weren't. He and Lidda were lost. They'd thought they were going back to the bottom of the shaft but must have gone deeper into the labyrinthine cave. Regdar and Naull could be alive, like them, but lost. There might be miles of caves. They might never find each other, might never find their way out.

Jozan began to whisper, "Pelor grant me the wisdom—"

Lidda had to reach up way over her head to clamp a cold hand over his mouth, but she managed it. He looked down at her, and she held a finger to her lips, her sword dangling upside down in that hand. Her eyes darted away, in the direction of the web, and Jozan could have sworn one of her ears actually twitched like a dog's.

He nodded once, and she took her hand away, then brought her sword back up and slid the lantern off the loop at her belt. She set the light down on the cave floor and seemed to almost sink into the side of a stalagmite. It was all Jozan could do to keep track of her slow, deliberate movement as she crept ever closer to the web.

Not sure what to do, he stood next to the lantern and waited.

The sound of that pained, desperate wail washed over him. It was the voice Lidda had mistaken for Regdar's, and it was coming from the web.

Jozan closed his eyes and tried to center himself, hoping to wrap himself in the reassuring presence of Pelor, but he could feel his hands shaking. He hated that sound.

There was a grunt that broke through the low wail, stopping it cold and sending echoes of the two sounds passing each other from cave wall to cave wall. There was a growl that Jozan thought might be Lidda, then another growl, then two rumbling grunts. It sounded like voices—muffled, heard from far away through intervening walls.

Jozan scooped up the lantern and dared to whisper, "Lidda?"

There were two more grunts, then Lidda called back, "Jozan, up here."

The priest held the lantern high in front of him and did his best to follow the sound of the halfling's voice. In the time it took for him to find her, standing in front of a wall of webbing, there were at least three more of the grunting couplets, and Jozan realized that Lidda was speaking to someone.

The halfling barked out two harsh, nonsensical growls, then turned to Jozan as he slipped past a stalagmite to stand next to her. A tear traced a curving path down one of the halfling's dirty cheeks. Her eyes were red, and her face was quivering.

"Jozan," she said, "you have to help him."

She turned away, and Jozan followed her gaze to the wall of webs. Stuck there, hanging nearly upside down, its right arm twisted behind its back at such an extreme angle that its shoulder joint, obviously dislocated, bulged under its pale yellow skin, was a goblin—and it was alive.

"His name is—" Lidda barked out a harsh grunt that sounded like it might have begun and ended with a "k" sound.

Jozan studied the goblin. Its—his—skin was wrinkled, and there were splotches of orange and muddy brown showing through its tissue paper surface. Age spots, Jozan assumed. The goblin looked up at him with one bulging, cloudy eye. His other eye was swollen closed, a gray bruise flowering around it.

Lidda pronounced the goblin's name again, more slowly, and Jozan repeated, "Klnk."

"He is chief of the Cavemouth Tribe," Lidda said.

"You speak their language?" Jozan asked her, still looking at the pitiful old goblin. "You never told us that."

"Can you help him?" she asked, ignoring his question.

Jozan hung his mace on his back and crouched down in front of the restrained goblin. He reached out but stopped just short of touching the web. The strands were fine, at least compared to the spidersilk strands of the rope ladder he'd climbed down earlier. The spider that made this web was smaller.

"If we can get him out of the web," Jozan said, "I can try."

"You healed Regdar," she said.

He turned to look at her. Though he was crouching, he looked the little halfling in the eye.

"I can do that again," he said, "but it will mean one less of another spell."

Lidda drew in a breath. She was probably going to ask him what other spell might be more important, or tell him that the old goblin wouldn't last long enough to debate it, but she stopped herself.

"You have a dagger," the priest said. "We should try to cut him loose."

She reached to her belt, then visibly sagged. "I threw it," she said. "It's still stuck in the—"

She looked at the old goblin, whose one eye rolled up to meet her gaze. The goblin barked out two grunts, then two more, then two more. Lidda listened with narrowed eyes, then grunted herself twice. Jozan couldn't imagine that was really a language, that ideas could be transferred with these simplistic, guttural vocalizations.

"What did he say?" Jozan asked.

"They keep the spiders for food and . . ." she said, shaking her head. "I'm not sure, maybe something like 'livestock'? The spiders turned on them, because of something another goblin tribe did."

Jozan said, "Keep talking. Find out as much as you can while I try to figure out how to get him down."

It took the better part of an hour, but Jozan, using the lantern flame to make a tiny torch out of a broken crossbow bolt, managed to get the old goblin out of the web. As he worked, Lidda grunted her way through a halting conversation with the dying humanoid. Jozan brought to mind the prayer that would help him replace one spell with another that would at least begin to heal the goblin's grievous wounds.

When the old goblin was laying still but alive on the floor of the cave, Lidda said, "He's speaking a funny dialect and can't manage the sign language, but I think what happened was—"

She stopped short when a spider appeared as if from nowhere. Jozan went sprawling backward from his crouching position to clatter onto the floor. The creature was on top of the old goblin, and before either Jozan or Lidda could react, it sank its sharp fangs into the old goblin's chest. There was an awful wet, cracking sound, and the goblin let loose another low, long, echoing wail.

Jozan fumbled for his mace while trying to kick the spider, but he was at an odd angle, wrapped up in his own armor like a turtle rolled on its back. The old goblin went limp, and Jozan knew he was dead. There was a flash of reflected light, and Lidda's sword came down at the spider. The thing released its grip on the dead goblin and launched itself backward with all eight legs. Lidda's blade sank an inch into the already dead goblin, where the spider had just been. The halfling barked out a curse that, under normal circumstances, would have made Jozan blush.

Instead, he scrambled to his feet and managed to get his mace in front of his body just as the spider leaped at him. It smashed into the mace, and it took all of Jozan's strength to keep the weapon from rebounding into his own forehead. The enormous brown spider wrapped its legs around the weapon and clapped its mandibles together, snapping at Jozan's face.

The priest almost threw his weapon away, then he saw Lidda skip in front of him, dragging her blade along the spider's back as she went. There was a splash of yellow ichor, and the spider dropped off the mace.

Jozan couldn't help but smile. There was something reassuring in Lidda's reaction to the spider on his mace. It was like something Regdar would do.

He looked over to her and said, "Thank you, L—"

"By the Protector," Lidda interrupted, still holding her short sword in both hands, looking up into the darkness. "We need to run away—as fast as we can."

Jozan looked around and saw shadows move and come together and pass through each other. The webs were waving as if in a stiff breeze.

"Spiders," he whispered.

Lidda grabbed him by the arm and pulled, shouting, "Lot's of 'em—*let's go!*"

Regdar hopped up and down in the cold water, moving gradually to his left, but all he felt above him was the same smooth rock. He kept his eyes closed and tried not to imagine what might be in the water with him. His chest burned, his throat burned, his eyes burned . . . he had less than a minute to live. Regdar was determined to spend that time trying to save his life.

When the darkness behind his eyelids turned glowing red, Regdar was sure he was dying. Was that Pelor's light? Was it his time to pass into the embrace of—

No, he thought, don't give up.

Regdar opened his eyes, and there was a shaft of bright light in the water with him. He could see everything all at once: the water, clearer than any he'd ever seen; the smooth gray-white rock above his head; the slivers of black fish no longer than his thumb; and the surface of the water in front of him.

The shaft of light bounced up and down, and Regdar could see that it was a staff of wood that was somehow glowing with a cold white light. He reached out and grabbed it, and someone pulled the staff up. It slipped out of his hand, but he bounced after it, coming out from under the little ledge that might have been his tomb for the fact that he didn't know that air was two steps in front of him.

He pushed off the bottom and grabbed the staff again. When his head came out of the water he drew in a deep breath, and his head spun. It was the finest air he'd ever breathed.

"Thank the Lord of All Magics," Naull said. "I thought you were going to drown."

Regdar reached out and with Naull's help managed to get a firm hold on the side of the clear pool. He coughed, hearing and feeling a little water rattle in his throat. He crawled the rest of the way out of the pool. Regdar was shivering and self-conscious in front of the young woman.

He saw that they were in a small chamber at the foot of another waterfall. His eyes settled on Naull's plain wooden staff, aglow with obviously magical light.

"If you . . . could do that," he said, still panting for air, "why . . . were we . . . fumbling around with that damn torch?"

Naull opened her mouth to form an excuse but burst out laughing instead. Regdar laughed with her.

The caves of the Stonedeep Tribe were cut from solid rock by forces Tzrg couldn't begin to fathom. Goblins moved into the tunnels a long time ago, but the caves were ancient even then. It was as close to a perfect environment as any goblin could ask for, but it was not without its idiosyncrasies—even dangers. The caves held many surprises for anyone who wasn't careful where he stepped, even if he could see in the dark.

Only steps from the *ksr* pit was one of the cave's most dangerous places: a sheer drop-off as tall as ten goblins. It was as if the floor of the cave just fell away.

A stairway of piled stones had been constructed along one wall so the goblins could move from the *ksr* pit and the higher caves down into the deeper chambers where the tribe made its nests and kept its females and young. The stairway was just wide enough for two goblins to climb it side by side. The cliff stretched the whole way across the width of the cave—lots more than eighteen feet across.

Rezrex had ordered a number of torches to be lit. They were held by Stonedeep warriors, stuck in cracks on the floor and walls, and propped between stones on the stairway. Hive spiders scurried in and out of the flickering shadows, the *tap-tap-tap* of their feet mingling with the echoes of goblin voices that filled the chamber. The ceiling was so high that Tzrg had never actually seen it, though he knew it was up there, in the reassuring darkness.

The captured goblins were brought out in groups of five tied to each other by thick queen spidersilk. The whole of Stonedeep Tribe—even the females and young—was gathered around them, with Rezrex watching the whole thing from the top of the tall ledge. Behind the hobgoblin was the *ksr* pit, in front of him, the cliff. The Stonedeep goblins gathered at the foot of the drop-off, most of them staring up at the hobgoblin with frightened reverence.

Rezrex's hobgoblin cronies and a few of the Stonedeep goblins hurried the prisoners along, pushing and prodding at them with hands and the sharp points of javelins until they were lined up, more than eighteen of them in all, along the edge. Most of the captive goblins looked scared, and Tzrg couldn't help thinking that those were the smart ones. He watched Rezrex pacing back and forth behind them, huge arms crossed in front of him, the extraordinary mace swinging from a strap at his back. He held his chin up high in a way that Tzrg had never seen before. There was something about the way the hobgoblin carried himself, not just his size, that commanded obedience.

"You left your females behind," the hobgoblin said, his voice so loud in the high-ceilinged chamber Tzrg wanted to put his hands over his ears.

The Cavemouth goblins looked down at the floor, most of them purposefully avoiding looking over the edge of the tall drop-off. Tzrg scanned the line of prisoners, ignoring the hive spiders that scuttled across the wall under them, confused by the gathering.

One of the Cavemouth prisoners wasn't looking down. Tzrg recognized him—his name was Glnk. He'd seen the other prisoners defer to him. Was Glnk their chief, then? Tzrg thought the Cavemouth Tribe's chief was Klnk—a much older goblin than this Glnk. If Glnk was their chief now, his defiance made Tzrg feel weak enough, if he wasn't the chief, he made Tzrg feel even weaker. It looked like Glnk was going to stand up to the hobgoblin, which was something Tzrg—the Stonedeep Tribe's legitimate chief—couldn't do.

"There is no more Cavemouth Tribe!" Rezrex roared.

His hobgoblin henchmen laughed, nodding and sneering at the prisoners. A murmur spread through the Stonedeep goblins, and some faces turned toward Tzrg. He winced and looked down at the floor, then realized that he should get them to look at Rezrex. Rezrex was the chief and would always be the chief. They needed to stop looking to him for anything. Tzrg was just a goblin, just a warrior, just a servant of the hobgoblin invader—just like everyone else.

Tzrg turned his chin up to look at Rezrex. The hobgoblin was pacing behind the Cavemouth prisoners, towering over them, looking down at them with that uncanny self-assurance that Tzrg was sure he'd never have himself, even if he was twice as big.

The hobgoblin caught Tzrg's eye and lifted one eyebrow. Tzrg's blood ran cold, but he twisted his face into a toothy smile and pumped both fists in the air. His arms felt as heavy as flowstone, but when he saw the corner of Rezrex's mouth curl up and the hobgoblin looked away, he knew Rezrex had fallen for it.

The hobgoblin turned his attention back to the prisoners, and Tzrg let his hands fall back down to his side. He watched Glnk, who was in the middle of a group of five prisoners with two tied to each side of him. Glnk kept his chin held high, while his tribemates were trying desperately not to meet the hobgoblin's gaze.

One of the prisoners tied to Glnk glanced at the defiant goblin, then forced his chin up. The second goblin tied directly to Glnk swallowed hard, then did the same. The three goblins, two of them emboldened by Glnk's courage, gazed directly at Rezrex as if challenging the hobgoblin to notice them.

But Rezrex didn't notice them, at least not at first. The hobgoblin was too busy scanning the reactions of the Stonedeep Tribe.

"There is only one tribe now," Rezrex announced. The hobgoblin was beginning to master the sign and body language that made Goblin a more expressive language. "There is only one tribe, and I am your chief."

A cheer rose up from the Stonedeep Tribe, and Rezrex grinned, soaking it in. He continued to pace back and forth behind the prisoners, his arms still folded in front of his chest. The goblins he passed behind flinched when he came close. They were afraid of being pushed off the edge. Tzrg had fallen farther into the water, but there was no water under these goblins, just a hard death on even harder stone.

"Bring your females down here," Rezrex commanded. "Join the one tribe and march with me to unite all goblin tribes. All of them! Everywhere!"

Another cheer went up, and Tzrg cringed again. How could anyone imagine such a thing?

A few of the Cavemouth prisoners looked up but kept their heads down. The lines on their faces softened, and they looked less frightened, almost relieved. More than one head turned slowly but deliberately to their leader.

This, Rezrex noticed. Tzrg watched Rezrex follow the prisoners' gazes to Glnk, who stood between two of his tribemates, heads held high, looking up to make eye contact with the huge hobgoblin.

Rezrex smiled and said, "You have something to say?"

"Cavemouth fights," the defiant prisoner said.

Tzrg sighed. He had to respect this goblin who had more guts than sense. Rezrex would kill him—maybe quickly by pushing him off the cliff, maybe slowly in the *ksr* pit. It was the certainty of that fate that had compelled Tzrg to surrender his own tribe, weeks before.

Any thought that the Cavemouth chief would follow Tzrg's example faded when Glnk said, "Hobgoblin dies."

One of the two goblins standing next to the foolish chief smiled and actually had the audacity to laugh. Rezrex laughed with him, his huge, deep, hearty guffaw drowning out the goblin's defiant cackle.

The hobgoblin strolled over to the laughing goblin, who stood tied to Glnk and three more of his tribemates. Glnk started to laugh as well. Other goblins, among both tribes, glanced nervously at their neighbors and began forcing smiles, ready to laugh along with them.

Rezrex still seemed too far away to reach the laughing goblins, but his foot shot out and pushed Glnk off the edge. Any trace of laughter echoed away and there was only silence for the half a heartbeat it took for the spidersilk ropes to tighten. The Cavemouth chief swung back into the face of the stone cliff and smashed against it with enough force to drive the air from his lungs in a resounding grunt.

The two goblins on each side of him grunted as well, and grabbed for the ropes that tied them to the fallen goblin and that kept him from falling to his death. They both had to take at least a step closer to the edge. The goblin on the left grimaced, and Tzrg could see the muscles in his arms bulge so that veins traced meandering paths under his dull orange skin. The goblin on the right took another step closer to the edge, obviously not as strong as his tribemate.

One of Rezrex's hobgoblin cronies stepped forward, grinning, and was going to push the weaker goblin over the edge. Rezrex put out a hand to stop his henchman. They exchanged words in their complex language, and Rezrex reached to the hobgoblin's side. He wrapped his hand around the pommel of the hobgoblin's sword and drew the rusted steel weapon from its scabbard.

The shrill sound echoed, startling the struggling, weaker goblin just enough to send him over the edge. He swung a bit farther out, and while he was still in the air, swinging down and back in on a collision course with Glnk, Rezrex brought the sword down in a hard chop that severed the web between the falling goblin and the one next to him, who was still on his feet at the top of the drop-off. There was a loud, collective gasp from all the goblins, Cavemouth and Stonedeep alike, when Rezrex brought the sword across and out to his right.

The blade bit through the web rope that secured the already dangling chief to his falling friend. The goblin screamed on the way down. His scream was joined by a dozen or more others, mostly from the Stonedeep females. When he hit the cave floor blood splashed onto the first row of Stonedeep goblins, sending them pushing backward into their tribemates. Tzrg, standing closer to the back, only barely felt the wave push into him as the crowd withdrew from the bloody sight.

Glnk, still dangling off the edge of the drop-off, shouted a name Tzrg presumed belonged to the bloody mess at the bottom of the cliff.

Rezrex reached down and grabbed the rope. He pulled up, leaning back a little, and dragged Glnk back onto the top of the cliff.

"Will you bring your females?" Rezrex demanded of the dazed, angry, grief-stricken goblin.

Glnk didn't answer at first, so Rezrex rolled his bodyguard's sword through his fingers and set the point under the still shaken goblin's chin.

"Females," the hobgoblin repeated, his brows turning down over his nose, his eyes burning in the torchlight.

The goblin met Rezrex's cold stare and said, "No."

Tzrg recognized the word. It was a hobgoblin word that Rezrex used a lot.

"No," the hobgoblin snorted, pulling Glnk to his feet. "You know what a *ksr* is, Glnk?"

There were noises behind them—at least Jozan thought the noises were behind them. In the confines of the cave, however deep underground they were, every little sound bounced off unseen walls and seemed to come from every direction at once.

It was hard to see any details as they ran. There were signs of goblin habitation all around them, but he didn't pause long enough to soak it in. They made tools from wood they obviously collected from the surface, as well as the stone and parts of dead spiders they had all around them in the caves.

The stalagmites thinned out considerably, and it was easier to run. Jozan was surprised at his own speed. The cool air rushed past his ears. Lidda was a blur next to him.

"Are they chasing us?" she asked, her voice blowing past him like wind.

Jozan stumbled trying to stop, but only managed to slow down a little. He was running downhill and hadn't even realized it. They'd been going deeper for a while, blindly fleeing the spiders that might not even be chasing them after all. His face flushed, and he would have felt foolish if he wasn't so busy feeling like such a coward.

"Stop," he said, as much to himself as to Lidda.

He finally skidded to a halt. The halfling was already standing still, waiting for him. Her lantern swung at her side, but the light seemed dimmer.

"What's wrong?" she asked.

He was panting like a dog, and she was barely breathing at all. He resisted the temptation to remind her that he was wearing armor, and that—

"Jozie?" she asked, eyes wide. "You all right?"

He cleared his throat, wiping his forehead with a metal-gauntleted hand.

"I'm fine," he said. "We have to stop, though. We're going deeper."

"I know," she said, "but the spiders . . ."

"The spiders might not even be following us," Jozan said, turning to peer into the darkness from which they'd come. He slid the mace off his back and held it ready in case the spiders were coming. "We should find a way back up, and . . . what did you call me?"

The halfling didn't answer. He turned to look at her and saw her carefully filling her lamp from a flask of oil. The light grew slowly brighter.

"Lidda," he said, "did you hear me?"

She looked up at him and said, "What, now?"

"What did you call me just then?"

"What?"

"I'm not Regdar," the priest said. "I'm not to be trifled with, child."

Lidda's eyes narrowed, and she looked at him as if she wasn't sure what language he was speaking.

"Sorry," she said, as insincerely as Jozan had ever heard anyone say anything.

He turned and looked back into the darkness behind them again. Still no spiders.

"They kept the spiders like cattle or something," she said. "Another tribe of goblins came and did something bad—I'm not sure what—that made the spiders turn on them."

Jozan turned back to her and said, "I beg your pardon?"

"The old goblin, Klnk," she said with a shrug. "He tried to tell me what was going on, but I didn't catch all of it. He said his son went after them but never came back."

Jozan sighed and reached up to take off his helm. If he had taken it off a second before, he might have been knocked out when the rock hit him in the head.

There was a loud clang, and he saw Lidda's eyes widen in surprise. He blinked a couple times, and his head hurt. There was a strange sound echoing through the cave, a loud, shrill, ululating sound that only made his head hurt more. He turned, ignoring a series of loud grumbling grunts from the halfling behind him.

The shadows moved, and as Jozan's head cleared, he brought his mace up. There was a group of squat little humanoids—goblins, but different somehow—and they were making the strange noise. One of them threw a rock, but it flew wide of its intended target, which was Jozan's head.

Lidda brushed past him. As she did, the light from her lantern fell on the goblins, and Jozan realized they were female. Dressed in tatters of cast-off clothing, some of them clutching squirming yellow infants to their breasts, they hopped up and down, brandishing rocks and making that strange noise.

"Oh, for Pelor's sake," Jozan murmured.

Lidda held her hands in front of her, showing her empty palms to the crowd of female goblins. They scuttled back to avoid her even as she grunted at them in what Jozan had come to recognize as their primitive language.

"Tell them we mean them no harm," he said.

Another rock launched out of the crowd at him, and he batted it away with his mace just in time to avoid it smashing his face in.

"And tell them to stop throwing rocks at me!"

Lidda was trying to say something to them, but Jozan could tell by the way they kept up their high-pitched chant and bent to pick up more rocks that they weren't listening.

Regdar and Naull managed to find a dry torch and light it before the effects of the light spell wore off. Drying everything out, though, was a lost cause, and Regdar grimly accepted the fact that he was going to be wet and cold for a long time. He certainly wasn't about to take off his armor. Regdar found no small consolation, though, in the fact that they seemed to have managed to keep hold of everything they fell into the water with—or, at least, everything that fell in with them.

They both looked up at the waterfall, which disappeared into the darkness above. Its source was far above the reach of Regdar's feeble torchlight, but he could see enough to realize that they would have to find a different way out. Even if Naull could climb as well as he could, they would have to work against falling water the whole way. The fact that they had gotten hopelessly turned around in the first fall was enough for Regdar to admit to himself that even if they could manage the climb, they would still be lost.

He turned to face the only other way out of the chamber: a dark mouth that emptied into a high-ceilinged cave, the floor of which sloped a bit downward. They'd be going deeper, but they'd be going somewhere. On his left, another, smaller waterfall, splashed into a second pool.

"Do you think there's any way Jozan and Lidda could find us?" Naull asked, her voice ricocheting from the rough stone walls. "Maybe there's only this one way down."

Regdar shrugged, turning away, and didn't tell her what he really thought.

"We should find another way out," he said. "Once we're back on the surface, we can find the pit we climbed down. Jozan and Lidda might be waiting for us there."

"You think they'd leave without us?"

"I hope so," he said.

She gave him an odd look, and he turned away again.

"We should go," he said. "It looks like there's only one way—"

Naull hissed at him and touched him on the arm. Her head was cocked to one side, and her face had drained of what little color the cold water had left her. Regdar put a hand on the hilt of his sword but didn't draw it. He listened, but all he heard at first was the echoing rush and spatter of the waterfalls. Naull pulled gently on his arm and turned to face him. Regdar bent slightly at the waist, bringing his ear close to her upturned face. He felt his skin tingle when her breath touched the side of his neck.

"I hear voices," she whispered, then glanced at the dark cave mouth.

Regdar straightened and took a few slow, silent steps toward the cave mouth. He bent a little closer and finally heard what Naull had described as voices. To Regdar they sounded more like grunts. He was put in the mind of pigs but couldn't imagine they'd run across any pigs the gods knew how deep underground.

Naull stepped up next to him, standing very close. He could feel her anxiety but had no idea how to reassure her. If there was something grunting down that tunnel, they were going to have to run into it sooner or later. It was their only way out.

He bent down to whisper in her ear and could see her tense as he came in close.

"We have to see what it is," he said. "Stay close behind me."

Standing, he drew his sword as slowly and as quietly as he could, not waiting for an answer from Naull. Regdar felt better with his sword in his hand. Holding the torch out in front of him, he slid up to the ragged stone wall to his right. He reached back to motion Naull to follow his lead, and the young mage complied. They started moving slowly, as quietly as they could under the less-than-favorable circumstances, and found that the floor sloped rather less severely at the edge. There were a few stalagmites to hang on to as they went, and as slowly as they walked they both managed to get onto level ground without slipping.

The tunnel was about twenty-five feet wide where it emptied into the chamber. The ceiling was still too far over their heads to see. To Regdar it seemed as if they were traveling in a bubble of dull orange torchlight, with nothing around them on all sides but utter blackness. He found it unsettling, but the presence of the young mage was somehow comforting. She was certainly more nervous than he was—he could see her hands shaking and the tight-set line of her jaw—but at least he wasn't alone. Though he rarely sought refuge in idle chatter, he wished he could speak to her, but with the grunting and snorting sounds echoing ever more loudly—ever more closely—in front of them, he kept his mouth shut.

When he almost fell over a sudden drop-off, he cursed his wandering thoughts. His foot dangled in midair for a heart-stopping moment before he drew back, pushing Naull gently away with his broad back. He swung his torch slowly in front of him.

There was a deep depression in the side of the tunnel, a good four feet deeper than Regdar was tall. The floor fell away all at once in an irregular line. Below was the dark mouth of a side-passage. Regdar bent forward a bit farther, trying to listen down the much more confined space.

He turned back to Naull, who was gazing at him expectantly, and whispered, "I don't think the sounds are coming from there."

He was being honest but was secretly worried that maybe he was hearing what he wanted to hear. Regdar wasn't the slightest bit pleased with the idea of climbing down into an even smaller, tighter space.

He could see Naull trying to listen, and after a bit she nodded and whispered, "It's straight ahead. What is it?"

Regdar shrugged. He could hear the grunting sounds much more clearly, the echoing hiss of the waterfalls behind him only barely audible.

He held his torch out to the side and walked carefully, still trying to be as quiet as he could. Naull grabbed hold of his armor and walked just as carefully behind him. Together they traced the outline of the drop-off and finally came back to the jagged stone wall.

They continued following the wall for maybe twenty or thirty feet before Naull, still holding Regdar's tassets, whispered, "Wait."

The fighter stopped and was about to turn around but stopped himself. Instead, he swiveled his head, so she wouldn't let go.

"Won't it be able to see the torch?" she asked.

It took Regdar a moment or two to sort out what she meant, but when he did, his face flushed. They were walking through pitch darkness with a lit torch. They could tiptoe all they wanted, but if whatever it was that was grunting had eyes, they'd be as obvious as a roc in a birdbath.

"Can you cast a spell to . . . ?" Regdar wasn't sure what he hoped a spell might do for them.

Naull shook her head and looked at him imploringly.

He had no idea what to do. They couldn't see in the dark. They had to have the torch. If it was a lantern they might be able to shield it somehow, but a torch . . .

"We have no choice," he whispered.

Naull looked like she was going to say something but didn't.

He turned back and kept moving along the wall, Naull still in tow.

They stopped when the edge of the torchlight revealed a narrowing of the tunnel ahead of them. The grunting noises came intermittently, echoing, but clearly in front of them. To the right, the wall they'd been following curved outward and wrapped around a pool of clear water so still Regdar couldn't tell if he was seeing stalagmites jutting up from the pool's bottom or reflections of the stalactites hanging above it. The tunnel narrowed to less than ten feet, though the ceiling was still too high above them to see. To the left, Regdar could barely make out what might have been another side-passage. He motioned Naull forward then crossed to the other side, hugging the left wall with the torch, his sword arm away from the rock in hopes of both hiding the torchlight and giving him more room to fight.

The cave continued to widen, then the wall curved back inward, and Regdar stopped again. Across the passage and forward was another pool of still, clear water, and deeper in was the unmistakable orange glow of torchlight.

"Do you see that?" Regdar whispered.

Torches meant at least some civilization. Even if it was only goblins living there, they might convince the humanoids—one way or another—to show them the way out.

Naull nodded and replied, "Put your torch out."

Excited, Regdar tossed his torch into the pool across the narrow tunnel.

Even as it sailed through the air, Regdar cringed and almost cursed aloud. When the flame hit the cold water with a deafening hiss followed by the torch's resounding splash, he actually whispered, "Damn it," and pressed his back against the stone wall.

Naull followed his lead, and both of them were keenly aware that the grunting noises had abruptly stopped.

Sure that whatever it was knew they were there, it occurred to Regdar that he should just run in and get it—whatever "it" might be—over with, but he had to think of Naull. If he went down fighting because he'd prematurely revealed himself to an enemy, that would be one thing, but to bring Naull with him . . .

Before Regdar could continue wrestling with this dilemma, the grunting noises began again.

"It's got to be goblins," Naull whispered.

Regdar turned to her and could see the impatience in her face. She curled both hands around her staff and nodded once, sharply, toward the torchlight.

Regdar waved her back then leaned forward and to his right to peer around the cave wall.

From where he stood, Regdar could see a pool of light cast by a torch that had been set into a crack in the right-hand wall, about ten feet past the edge of the second pool—about forty feet all together from Regdar. Between the far edge of the pool and the torch was a cage constructed of broken-off stalactites held together by what looked like the same thick spidersilk as the rope ladder. A spider identical to the ones they'd fought on the surface picked its way along the dome-shaped top of the stone cage as if it was testing the spidersilk ties. Inside, cowering in the half of the cage floor closest to the wall, was a tightly pressed group of goblins.

The little creatures looked even more ragged than the goblins they'd seen before. What clothes they wore were rarely more than strips of torn cloth. Most if not all of them were wounded in some way—at least the odd scrape or gray-orange bruise—and none of them were armed.

Regdar assumed that they either hadn't heard his torch go out or didn't care. They were all looking away. He motioned Naull to look, and she slid up next to him close enough that he could feel her trembling.

Beyond the first cage was one more, and Regdar thought he could see just the edge of a third. A second torch burned even farther down, and Regdar thought there might be another pool along the right-hand wall just past the farther cages. In the second cage was another group of goblins. Regdar couldn't make out details, but something about the way they clustered to the far end of the cage made him think that they were in no better shape either physically or mentally than the goblins in the cage closer to him.

"More spiders," Naull whispered.

Regdar followed her gaze to the space between the two cages, where two of the huge spiders were wandering across the uneven floor. They disappeared from sight to the left. Regdar was about to ask Naull if she thought it was possible that the spiders were keeping the goblins captive—maybe as retribution for killing them and using their bodies to make bowls and tools—when the caged goblins murmured, grunted, and cowered even lower in their cages.

Regdar heard more of the guttural grunts and realized that they had been hearing voices after all, just voices speaking the primitive language of the subterranean humanoids.

"What's going on?" Naull asked.

"The jailer's coming," Regdar guessed, eyes glued to the cages.

Regdar hoped that he'd see a human approach the cages. He hoped it was anyone he might be able to talk to. Regdar didn't really care why the goblins were in cages. His limited experience of them had been generally negative, and he'd never heard a kind word spoken of the nasty little creatures. Regdar hoped that whoever was holding them would be good enough to show them the way out, but his more rational side knew that the chance of that was remote at best. The chances were better that whoever—or whatever—was holding the goblins prisoner would be even worse.

His answer came soon enough, when shadows flickered across the stone floor and the sound of shuffling footsteps echoed through the cave. Regdar crossed the fingers of his left hand, feebly hoping to see anything but—

—a goblin.

The jailer was another goblin and one that looked no more civilized than its prisoners. This one was armed, though, and brought one of its friends with it.

The jailer barked out unintelligible commands at the caged goblins, and its comrade stepped up to slice open some of the spidersilk with a rusty old dagger. The spider that had been skittering about the top of the cage turned and crawled down toward the now open cage with some determination. Two of the armed goblins went into the cage and dragged one of the prisoners out.

This goblin looked particularly abused, but there was something about the set of its shoulders and the way it made the jailers work to move it, that was almost impressive to Regdar. Its fellow goblins cowered only lower still. When the jailers turned their charge in Regdar's direction, the fighter was sure he saw a look of stern disappointment, even contempt, on the stiff prisoner's face.

The jailers dragged the goblin away, and the spider set immediately to work repairing the webs holding the cage closed. None of the goblin prisoners made a move to escape.

Regdar turned to Naull and said, "We're following them."

The rock spanked off the cave floor and shot up under Jozan's scale mail kilt, hitting him in the groin hard enough to double him over. He managed to remain on his feet, but he had to close his eyes and work to keep from throwing up. It crossed his mind that if he asked nicely, Pelor might take him into the next life right away.

"Hey!" Lidda cried, then grunted loudly at the goblin women in their primitive tongue.

Jozan heard three more rocks hit the floor near him, and he straightened up, blinking, only able to hope that he wouldn't get hit again. Lidda grabbed his arm and pulled hard enough to make him stumble.

"We should just leave," she said, her voice pitched even higher than normally and her face red in the lanternlight.

A stone bounced off her shoulder and she shouted, "Ow! What's it gonna take?"

Jozan turned and was finally able to take a deep breath. A stone bounced off his armored back, and he scowled. It was his turn to pull Lidda away from the growing crowd of feral goblin women.

"An eye?" she yelled at them even as she followed Jozan into the darkness. "Will that make you happy . . . when someone loses an eye?"

"Let's just go, child," Jozan hissed through clenched jaws. "They aren't what we're here for anyway, and they obviously don't want our—"

Jozan and Lidda leaped to either side when a short goblin javelin whizzed between them. The weapon clattered to a halt on the stone floor behind Jozan. Lidda, who was sitting on the cave floor, drew her sword and sprang to her feet.

Turning his attention to the source of the javelin, Jozan squinted into the darkness ahead. He tightened his grip on his mace and tried to think of a spell that might help them, but nothing he'd prayed for that morning would have been of immediate assistance.

A goblin stepped out of the darkness, then another right on the heels of the first. They both drew back their arms to hurl javelins. Ahead of him and to his left, Jozan saw a particularly fat, squat stalagmite—one that might provide cover from the javelins but that would also take him farther away from Lidda and the light of her lantern.

The goblins threw their javelins, and Jozan made up his mind. He ran toward the stalagmite, ducking a javelin on his way, and came to a skin-scraping halt behind it just as a second javelin clattered across the ground next to him.

"*Watch it!*" Lidda shouted, her voice an ear-piercing squeal.

He saw her making for similar cover, and when she passed behind a stalagmite, Jozan was thrust into almost total darkness. There was a pool of orange light ahead of him. He peeked over the top of the stalagmite and saw that one of the goblins—Jozan counted eight of them in all—was carrying a torch. They also seemed to have no shortage of javelins.

Jozan began to consider the odds against them when his face was pushed into the top of the stalagmite by a blow to the back of his head. He didn't hit hard, and neither did the rock—he doubted there'd be a dent in his helm—but it stung, reminding him that there was a threat from the rear as well.

The stone that hit him in the head bounced off and struck one of the advancing goblin warriors in the chest just hard enough to get its attention.

Jozan heard the telltale smack of stone on skin, then a deep, guttural grunt that couldn't have been Lidda. A goblin warrior charged him, and he stepped from behind the stalagmite with his mace at his side and back enough to put some momentum into a blow. Just as he was beginning to bring his arm forward to block the goblin's bent, rusted short sword, another rock flew past his head so closely he could hear it whistling through the air. The rock hit the charging goblin square in the face, and the little warrior dropped to the floor in a spinning flurry of arms and legs.

Jozan tried to get out of the fallen goblin's way but got tripped up in the thing's legs and went down hard, bouncing off the smooth, hard edge of the stalagmite that had been his cover.

He fell onto his back and saw more stones—at least four or five of them—shoot through the air over him. All but one bounced off a grunting goblin warrior and were followed by that ululating wail from the goblin females behind them.

"Looks like the ladies are on our side!" Lidda called from the darkness.

It took only a few whispered words for Regdar to determine that Naull wanted to follow the goblin jailers and their prisoner as much as he did. They were both at a loss as to how else to find their way out, and loath to get involved with what appeared to be a goblin prison. Regdar tried not to imagine what these goblins might have done that would cause other goblins—humanoids known to be particularly unpleasant—to lock them up.

The goblins had passed to their left, and Regdar couldn't see where they were going. Following them would mean walking right past the cages. Remembering that the caged goblins hadn't seemed to notice his torch going out, Regdar risked moving closer to get a better look.

Still hugging the cave wall to his right, he stepped up a good fifteen feet as quickly as he could without making too much noise. He peered around a corner to his left, just at the edge of the light from the torch stuck in the wall. The cave opened up into a large chamber with a floor that sloped rather precipitously downward. There were three cages full of goblins in all and another pool of water beyond them. The cave continued on past the pool and into darkness.

On the wall opposite the three cages was the black mouth of another side-passage. A torch was stuck in the wall near the entrance, a dim glow from inside the passage, the sound of goblins' grunting voices, and scuffling noises told Regdar that the goblins had gone that way.

He looked at the cages and saw that several goblin prisoners had finally noticed him. They were practically groveling, their mouths clamped tightly shut, their eyes bulging with what Regdar thought was surprise, mixed with fear.

The spider finished webbing the cage shut and scuttled off the stone bars and onto the floor.

When Naull touched his arm, Regdar jumped, scraping a pauldron on the wall. The sound was enough to startle the spider, and it turned on them, its row of black eyes glistening in the torchlight. It scuttled toward them quickly, and Regdar drew his arm back.

Naull started chanting in a quiet voice that still seemed like a roar in the otherwise quiet cave. Regdar ground his teeth and squinted, not sure what Naull was conjuring up but ready to smash the spider with his greatsword if she failed to stop it.

She stopped speaking, and as if on cue, the spider skittered to a halt, its striped, segmented legs ticking up underneath it, sending it rolling gently onto its back.

"It's asleep," Naull whispered, "but not for long."

Regdar released the breath he just then realized he was holding and said, "We need to risk it."

"Risk what?" she asked.

In lieu of an answer, Regdar took her thin forearm in his left hand and pulled her out with him into the torchlight. The goblin prisoners shifted back in response, but Regdar didn't wait to see what else they'd do. He pulled the young mage along behind him, across the treacherous sloping floor to the wall next to the side-passage.

He let go of Naull and whispered, "Take the torch."

She grabbed the torch that had been jammed into a crack in the wall next to the cave mouth and waited for Regdar to peek cautiously into the side-passage.

There was another torch set in the wall toward the back of the ragged cave. He could see that stalagmites had been cleared from the floor. Their round bases were like tree stumps. The ceiling was low enough to see and hung with slender stalactites that might brush the top of Regdar's helm. A gentle orange glow emanated from a hole in the cave floor and was slowly fading along with echoes of footsteps and the odd goblin grunt.

"Follow me," Regdar whispered and stepped into the side-passage.

At the edge of the hole, Regdar stopped and looked down. A rope ladder almost identical to the one they'd descended from the surface hung down into inky darkness. Naull stepped up to him and held the torch out over the hole. The floor was too far down for the torchlight to reveal.

Regdar knew that every second they hesitated meant the goblins would be farther ahead. If there were any more side-passages, intersections, or holes in the ground ahead of them, there would be no way to follow the goblins.

He looked at Naull, who was looking onto the dark pit with thin lips and shaking hands. She looked young, innocent, frightened, almost frail.

"Damn," she whispered.

Regdar blinked a couple times and said, "We could try something else if . . ."

She looked at him with anger in her eyes he hoped wasn't directed at him.

"Hold this," she said, thrusting the torch out toward him.

She crouched in front of the rope ladder, tested the knots where it was tied around the base of a broken-off stalagmite, and said, "They might be our only chance to find a way out of here or at least find out what's going on. I climbed before, I can climb again."

Regdar smiled and was surprised by a tightening in his throat.

"Wait," he said, then tossed the torch into the hole.

"What are you—?"

The torch fell maybe thirty feet before clattering to a stop on the cave floor below. The spidersilk ladder hung all the way to the floor. Naull breathed a sigh of relief that was so hard Regdar imagined he felt his whiskers riffle.

"After you," he said.

With a smile, Naull, started down the ladder. Regdar sheathed his sword, crouched, and steadied it for her. When she was almost to the floor, he swung down onto the ladder and was surprised to see that it held both their weight. In no time they stood on the floor of the narrow tunnel below. Naull bent to retrieve the torch.

They stood in silence, listening. At first there was nothing— just the sound of water dripping somewhere, the sound of their guttering torch, the sound of their own breathing, the sound of Regdar's heart beating.

When a grunt echoed around them, Naull drew in a breath. At first Regdar thought it had come from above, but Naull was pointing into the darkness. There was another grunt, then the clatter of steel on stone, and Regdar thought the mage might be right but couldn't be sure.

"This way," she said, her voice sounding more confident than her face looked.

"Are you sure?" he asked.

Naull looked up at him and shrugged. "Not really," she said. "This is my first time in a cave two thousand feet underground following goblins into a pitch-black tunnel that's probably full of huge spiders—you?"

Regdar blushed and stepped past her in the direction she'd indicated.

"No reason to be sarcastic," he grumbled, and instantly regretted it.

He was rewarded, though, by a quiet giggle from behind him. He smiled, knowing she couldn't see his face, and started walking faster.

"We should hurry, to gain ground on them," he said.

They followed the tunnel for a long time, passing one fork that briefly troubled them both. A quick detour showed them the error of their ways, and they only wasted a few minutes before finding the dead-end and going back.

When they saw the edge of the goblins' torchlight ahead of them, and the grunting voices came much more loudly, Regdar slowed and put a finger to his lips to tell Naull to be as quiet as she could.

The tunnel went on and on, and it was easy enough for them to keep the goblins just in sight in front of them. They were gradually moving upward, and Regdar was starting to feel as if they might be on their way out after all. The angle was slight, though, and he started to hope it would become more intense. At that angle he figured it might take them days to get all the way back to the surface.

As if designed to make him feel better, the cave floor did indeed start to rise at a greater angle. As they ascended, the sounds of goblin voices grew not only louder but decidedly more plentiful. Sounds of a struggle echoed down to them, followed by goblin shouts and what might have been a cheer.

Regdar stopped, listening, and the sounds didn't get any farther away.

"The tunnel must end up here somewhere," he whispered to Naull, who moved in close to him. "I think we—"

"Wait," she whispered, moving closer still. "I couldn't hear you."

She tilted her head and bent closer to Regdar. He leaned in and almost pressed his lips to her ear. He had the brief but uncomfortable notion that he should kiss her, but he pushed that aside. They were in danger, and there were more important things to think about than that, however good it made him feel.

There was something about the sounds that came echoing down the narrow tunnel that made Regdar stop, turn around, and walk out into the larger cave. The goblins were quiet, then they cheered, there was the shifting of rough cloth and the swish of bare feet on stone, the clicking of scuttling spiders, and underneath it, something big that was growling and moving on sharp claws.

Regdar, sensing Naull following close behind him, came out into an enormous cave. The colors washed past him in flowing white, gray, and brown. There were spears of stalactites hanging from the ceiling like enormous chandeliers. The floor had been made smooth and worn even smoother. He was standing on a natural platform twenty feet above the cave floor. Beyond the edge of the platform was a pit, as deep as the platform was high, but with one intermediary ledge like an inner ring or step that formed a simple but effective natural amphitheater.

On the floor of the pit was a creature Regdar had seen only once before and hoped never to see again. It was a hideous, man-eating beast called a krenshar. It growled and scraped its claws on the smooth stone floor of the pit, which was ringed by a crowd of maybe seventy goblins.

A ladder made of spidersilk ran from the edge of the platform to the outer edge of the pit, stretching diagonally like a crude staircase. At the foot of the web ladder, on the step above the floor of the krenshar pit, were the two goblin jailers and their prisoner.

"Regdar . . ." Naull whispered.

He could tell she was going to warn him off, but there was nothing she could say. Throwing someone—even a goblin—into a pit, defenseless, against a krenshar was just wrong.

Regdar charged down the spidersilk ladder, greatsword swinging behind him. The jailer to the left of the would-be krenshar victim turned. Its eyes widened and its mouth opened. The goblin brought its arm back, a crude stone club clenched in its hand.

Regdar spilled the goblin's entrails before it had time to scream.

A dead silence came over the cavern, and all heads turned to look up at Regdar. Mouths fell open, and there was a wave of gasps.

Regdar smiled and looked across the bizarre scene. On the other side of the pit sat a burly humanoid, much bigger than the goblins around him. It stood slowly and sneered at Regdar.

Hobgoblin, Regdar thought. I hate hobgoblins.

Behind the hobgoblin was another, but this one had a less impressive collection of trophies slung along its patchwork armor. Regdar noted a handful of the big brown spiders with the **X**s on their backs scattered among the goblins.

"Regdar," Naull called from up on the platform behind him, "what are we doing?"

The goblins panicked and ran in two big groups. Almost directly to Regdar's right, behind the prisoner and the surviving jailer, thirty goblins scrambled to their feet and practically crawled over each other to get away. They'd been sitting in a space between the pit and a sheer drop-off in the cave floor. By the light of torches stuck here and there in cracks in the walls and floor, Regdar could see a pile of large stones that had been fashioned into a crude stairway running down the drop-off. The thirty goblins made for the stone steps, some of the them slipping and falling—their comrades ran them right over.

The second group was half the size. They squeezed through narrow gaps in a stone wall across the pit from where Regdar was standing. The rock wall looked like a waterfall frozen in place.

The goblin prisoner, its hands tied behind its back, took advantage of the tribe's panic and pushed the surviving jailer-goblin hard with its shoulder and the side of its face. The jailer—a bit bigger than the rest of the goblins—tried to keep its balance by widening its stance. Unfortunately for the jailer, it was standing right at the edge of the pit. Its foot slipped over the edge, and the jailer tumbled fifteen feet into the krenshar pit.

Regdar stepped back and was just about to pull the prisoner into the narrow cave they'd come from when Naull, screaming, came flying through the air. Regdar realized she had been trying to jump on the jailer-goblin just as the prisoner pushed it into the pit.

Naull came to a hard, sliding stop on the step and slid off the edge. Regdar could see the fingers of both of Naull's hands, white and trembling as she held for dear life onto the sharp edge. He grabbed at the prisoner again, but the goblin spun on him and flinched away. The big hobgoblin roared twice in such a way that made Regdar think it was saying something to the two dozen or so goblins that hadn't run away.

In the pit, the krenshar charged the goblin jailer. The creature's razor-sharp claws shrieked across the smooth stone floor as it went. The goblin drew its dagger and screamed what might have been a challenge, a prayer, or just the incoherent cry of a goblin who knew it was about to die. It did step forward, though, and slashed its dagger down at the krenshar's head.

The smaller of the two hobgoblins charged around the perimeter of the krenshar pit, making its way toward Regdar with heavy, stomping feet. It was swinging a morningstar. The brutal weapon's two big steel balls, which were clustered with jagged spikes, whirled at the ends of heavy chains that hung from a leather-wrapped handle. The hobgoblin was almost exactly the same size as Regdar, who was ready for a decent fight. As the hobgoblin came around it sent two goblins tumbling into the krenshar pit and two more scrambling out of its way. It was only then that Regdar noticed the goblins cowering between the cave wall on his left and the edge of the krenshar pit.

The hobgoblin was moving slowly enough that Regdar could take the time to gently slice through the spidersilk holding the prisoner's hands behind its back. Behind the goblin he could see Naull's fingertips still clinging to the edge of the pit—then he turned back to see the hobgoblin coming at him fast and hard.

He had almost come to a snap decision about whether he would save Naull first or meet the hobgoblin's charge head on when a spider slammed into him. Its needlelike legs pinged off his armor, and the horrid sideways jaws clacked at him. It was all he could do to keep his left arm between the spider and his exposed face. The thing seemed to be trying to bite him in the eyes. Regdar could hear another one coming toward him from behind and up on the platform.

The bigger hobgoblin still stood at the other side of the pit, screaming a string of incoherent growls. By the sound of it, Regdar could tell the humanoid was angry—and getting angrier. In the pit there was the screech of claws on stone, then an ugly ripping noise and a pained, desperate wail—a goblin's wail.

The spider was crawling over Regdar's arm. He was twisting at the elbow and shoulder, trying to keep it off his face. Finally, he was able to get his huge greatsword inside and flicked a wedge out of the underside of the spider's brittle body. It quivered, convulsed, and its eight segmented legs curled up under its bleeding body, trapping Regdar's left arm with them. When the other spider leaped off the platform at him, Regdar used the dead spider on his arm like a shield and managed to avoid the thing's bite.

The block drew Regdar half a step sideways, and when he glanced down to make sure he wasn't too close to the edge, he saw the goblin prisoner, crouching low beneath him. The goblin snatched the stone club from the dead jailer.

The spider rolled off the dead one still stuck to Regdar's arm and came to rest on its feet, right next to the now-armed prisoner. There was a loud growl almost in Regdar's face, and he looked up just barely fast enough to see the hobgoblin almost upon him.

Regdar stepped backward and brought the dead spider up. The hobgoblin's morningstar smashed into it hard enough to rip it free of Regdar's arm and send it sailing up onto the stone platform above.

Regdar felt a hand on his ankle. He didn't risk a glance down, but was sure it was Naull. She pulled herself up and over the edge of the pit. Regdar could hear the krenshar's jaws snapping just below her. She whispered a curse and thanked the god of magic for her life.

The hobgoblin growled in Regdar's face and recovered quickly. Regdar ducked a backhand swing and brought his sword up to jab at the hobgoblin's midsection. The humanoid skipped back, letting its morningstar spin behind its head while it changed its grip on the weapon from one hand to the other. Regdar stepped in with a slash across the hobgoblin's chest that cut through its animal hide and bone armor, but not quite deeply enough to draw blood.

The goblin prisoner had to roll out of the way and hop up onto the space between the pit and the platform. The spider followed it, and Regdar caught just a glimpse of a splash of spider guts as the goblin prisoner broke through the spider's shell. Regdar could hear a third spider clattering up from behind him and hoped the ex-prisoner would take care of that one as quickly as it did the last.

The hobgoblin brought its morningstar down over its head with its left hand, and Regdar could see what it was trying to do. Its right hand was balled into a fist the size of a sledgehammer, and it was hoping Regdar would dodge the morningstar and move directly into the punch. Instead, Regdar dodged to the left and held his sword up over his head. The heavy steel balls wrapped the chain around Regdar's blade, and there was a second where the surprised hobgoblin stood there and watched it happen.

Regdar took that opportunity to look behind it. The goblins along the wall were watching in obviously stunned fascination. Behind the bigger, still ranting hobgoblin on the other side of the pit, a small group of goblins and a few of the spiders were rallying around a single goblin who was growling at them in that ugly language of theirs.

The big hobgoblin turned on them, and Regdar could see the fear in the eyes of all the goblins who had been rallying behind it. The sound of the big hobgoblin's voice was like thunder rolling through the huge cave. The thing was not happy.

The hobgoblin whose morningstar was wrapped around Regdar's sword kicked the human in the side hard enough to push the air out of his right lung. It was an odd, painful sensation, but Regdar didn't have time to stop and consider it. Tensing his right arm and bringing all of his considerable strength to bear, he twisted his greatsword out and to the left, flipping the morningstar from the hobgoblin's grip.

Doing so, though, turned him around, so that he had his back to the hobgoblin. Regdar was facing Naull's back and had to dodge to one side to avoid the young mage's staff. She jammed it back, then sliced it down, and Regdar watched it smash onto the top of a spider that was just about to bite her in the ankle. It was the spider Regdar had hoped the prisoner would kill—it was as if he'd forgotten about Naull completely. He drew in a breath, stunned and disappointed by the realization, only to be snapped back into the moment when the hobgoblin punched him in the back hard enough to rattle his teeth.

Regdar blinked and was oddly aware of the crowd of fleeing goblins pouring down the crude stone steps. Yet another spider was making its way toward him, and Regdar tried to ignore the sounds of two more goblins being ripped to pieces by the kren-shar.

The hobgoblin wrapped its huge, yellow-skinned arms around Regdar's head, and he knew the humanoid was going to try to break his neck. When the inevitable hard twisting motion came, Regdar rolled with it. His sword was too heavy with the morning-star still wrapped around it. As Regdar rolled to the side, slipping out of the hobgoblin's grip, he twitched his sword, so the chains would begin to unwind.

The hobgoblin must have realized that Regdar wasn't going to sit there and have his neck broken. It let go of Regdar's head and stepped back. The hobgoblin bumped into Regdar's back and growled in frustration, then something brushed past Regdar. It was the goblin prisoner. The little humanoid seemed to be scur-rying all over the place, getting in and under Regdar and the hob-goblin as if they weren't even there.

The goblin stood up just as it came by Regdar and reached out to grab at Naull. Regdar barked out a warning, but at the same time he heard the telltale squeak of a dagger being drawn somewhere just behind his head.

The goblin prisoner pushed Naull to the side, away from the pit, and Regdar could see the spider scurrying toward them. The prisoner brought its club down at the thing, but stopped a foot above it. The spider reacted anyway, hopping to one side. The goblin stomped down with its right foot and cracked three of the spider's legs, so they nearly broke off. The thing tried to jump away but only dragged its useless appendages a few inches before the goblin fell on it and killed it.

Naull took the opportunity to climb up and pass behind Regdar as if unaware of the life-and-death fight he was having with the hobgoblin. As he watched her pass he turned and stood. The morningstar slid off his sword, and Regdar kicked it into the pit at the same time he batted away the hobgoblin's long, serrated dagger.

Over the hobgoblin's shoulder Regdar saw the bigger humanoid barking more orders. This time, the goblins who had been content to watch started to work up their nerves. The little humanoids had weapons in their hands—javelins mostly, and heavy leg bone or stone clubs—and a strangely pathetic desperation in their eyes.

Regdar dropped his sword back and tensed for a hard slash that could end the hobgoblin when he heard Naull start to shout something that sounded like just the opposite of the goblins' guttural grunting. The words were lyrical and intricate, set in a chanting cadence that gave Regdar pause—just long enough for the hobgoblin to slash him across the hip with the big serrated dagger. It found a place between tassets and cuisse and ripped into his skin. Regdar clenched his teeth tightly together and held back a scream. Hot blood poured from the wound.

Jozan tried not to take satisfaction in the way it felt to crack
a goblin's skull with his bloody mace. He wasn't fighting for the
thrill of it—he wasn't even fighting to kill—but he had to defend
Lidda, the goblin females, and himself.

His eyes had become used to the dim light of Lidda's lantern,
and he was thankful that the halfling had stopped bouncing
around. The light was steady enough that he wasn't mistaking
shadows for goblins and vice versa. He couldn't see the little
thief, and she wasn't speaking, but the light was behind him and
to his right.

The goblin he'd just hit fell to one knee and put a hand to its
head, dropping the sharpened rock it had been using as a weapon.
Another of its comrades came up to jab at Jozan with a javelin, but
the priest stepped back, and the wounded goblin rolled over on its
side at the same time. The wounded goblin rolled onto the javelin-
wielder's feet, nearly tripping it. The javelin, instead of stabbing
Jozan, tipped upward. The priest took advantage of that and
stepped in to swat the weapon out of the goblin's hand. There was

a loud *snap!* and Jozan was pretty sure he'd broken one of the goblin's fingers in the process.

In response, the humanoid growled and gnashed its teeth like a mad dog. It stepped on its unconscious comrade and leaped at Jozan, apparently meaning to take down the priest with its bare hands.

Jozan closed his eyes, steeling himself against the inevitable impact. He'd overextended his mace knocking the javelin away and knew he couldn't get it back in front of him in time to backhand the diving goblin.

The impact never came. Instead, a gurgling whimper sounded in front of him. Jozan opened his eyes to see the goblin, blood dribbling from its slack-jawed mouth, slowly crumple to the floor on top of its fallen friend.

Lidda stood behind the goblin, blood oozing down the blade of her short sword.

There were at least three goblin warriors that Jozan could see behind her. They seemed as surprised to see the halfling as Jozan had been. The priest hadn't seen or heard her slip behind the goblin, though it explained why the lanternlight was so steady. She'd left it on the cave floor and slipped into the darkness.

The goblins turned and ran. Lidda started to turn to follow them, but Jozan managed to grab her shoulder. She stopped, turned her face to him, and winked.

Jozan sighed and said, "I was trying not to kill—"

There was a rapid series of feral grunts behind him, and Jozan turned to see the female goblins approaching them slowly, as if each step was painful for them. They stopped a good ten feet from the priest and the halfling, eyeing them and sniffing the cool, dank air.

Lidda stepped next to him and started growling and grumbling at them in their odd language. The females seemed hesitant to speak with her. Some in the back even picked up stones and tried to look threatening. Jozan, still sore between his legs, backed up a step.

Lidda sheathed her sword and showed her empty palms, grunting the whole time. Jozan followed suit, hanging his mace on his back and keeping both hands visible to the suspicious females. One of them stepped forward another couple steps and let loose a nonsensical stream of growling gibberish that Lidda listened to intently.

"I think they're telling us how to get out of here," Lidda finally whispered to Jozan.

"How?" the priest asked.

"She said we have to climb the water," replied Lidda.

"Climb the water?" Jozan asked. "What does that mean?"

Lidda barked at the goblin, who barked back and pointed into the darkness, roughly in the direction the warriors had fled.

"Not climb," Lidda said, more to herself than to Jozan. "Descend? *Mpktm bkn* . . . descend foreigner. *Mpktm gdv* . . . descend water. I think it's more like: 'You should descend the water' . . . or 'climb down the water' . . . right?"

"You're asking me?"

It was her most potent spell, though as spells go it was a simple one. Still, she had to concentrate hard to cast it. The intonation change from the second to the third quatrain was tricky and had to be accompanied by a Chienji Style left ring finger up-twist into the Awaiting Position while holding a pinch of red-colored sand between the thumb and little finger of her right hand, a pinch of yellow sand between the thumb and little finger of her left hand, and a pinch of blue sand between her right and left pointing fingers.

When the goblin they'd come to rescue brushed past her, Naull almost blew the spell. Out of the corner of her eye, she saw it scurry up the spidersilk ladder. It was obviously heading back up to the platform and the narrow tunnel beyond.

The big hobgoblin continued to bark orders at its cowardly charges. The humanoid turned, grabbing a goblin from behind and shouting into its face. Naull remained focused on her spell, though part of her mind wondered how bad the hobgoblin's breath must smell at that range.

She spoke the last syllable of the incantation and flipped both hands out and open, ejecting the sand into the air in front of her. The goblins who had been cowering along the wall were moving toward them, some with obvious evil intent glimmering in their otherwise dull eyes.

The burst of colored light that sprayed out from her fingertips made Naull blink. She was happy to see that she'd aimed the effect properly, missing Regdar. The blaze of flashing colored light swept over the approaching goblins, who had made the mistake of clustering together. The hobgoblin that was close to killing Regdar stood in the whirling cone of magic as well.

Naull felt like whooping with delight when every one of the goblins who'd been enmeshed in the light crumpled to the cave floor in twitching heaps. When the hobgoblin, serrated dagger raised for its killing blow, tumbled off the edge and into the pit, she almost burst into tears.

"*Yes!*" she exclaimed, forgetting herself.

The colored lights had already faded. The echoes of her single word bounced through the huge cavern, hissing through a sudden, complete, stunned silence.

Regdar watched the hobgoblin fall into the pit with a mixture of disappointment, relief, embarrassment, and envy. He would have liked to have killed the son of a bitch himself but wasn't sure he'd have been able to, though the goblins would only think him weaker for having been saved by a woman. He couldn't help wishing he could drop that many foes at once.

He moved half a step from the edge of the pit and scanned the cave. The hobgoblin hadn't so much fallen into the pit as slid. The big humanoid was leaned up against the smooth rock wall, propped up on the bloody corpse of one of the goblins that had already fallen victim to the krenshar.

And there was the monster. It put one front claw tentatively on the fallen hobgoblin, who Regdar realized was still breathing. When the precariously hanging hobgoblin didn't slide off the wall, the krenshar started to climb.

"Female saved you good, Man," the hobgoblin on the other side of the pit called.

Startled by the fact that the brute spoke Common, Regdar looked up, though he was still keenly aware of the approaching krenshar.

"Ksr . . ." the hobgoblin called, " . . . krenshar you call, yes? Krenshar not hide by wall, Man. Krenshar bite face off!"

The hobgoblin was still holding a goblin by its tattered tunic. It didn't seem to care that most of its warriors had run away, a whole phalanx of them had been dropped into what might have been a coma for all Regdar knew, and one of his own kind was acting as a ladder for a wild, vicious predator.

The krenshar was almost on him, so Regdar turned his attention away from the foolish hobgoblin. Movement up and to his left caught his eye, though, and he glanced up in time to see the former prisoner dashing across the rock platform obviously on its way to the tunnel.

Naull, who was still radiating well-deserved self-satisfaction looked up at the fleeing goblin as well.

Regdar, gluing his eyes to the krenshar, said, "Follow him. He might know the way out."

She glanced at him, then back up at the platform. Regdar could hear the prisoner's footsteps receding.

"Go," he said, and she started for the web ladder.

The krenshar got one foot over the edge of the pit, but Regdar wanted to wait until he could get a clear hack at the monster's head.

He spared a quick glance at Naull and was happy to see her on her way up the spidersilk ladder—then he saw the goblin.

Her spell must have missed one, and it was coming at her with its wicked little javelin out on front of it. Regdar shouted her name but probably didn't have to. Before the goblin could stab her with its javelin, she swung her staff down fast and hard, hitting the goblin on its shoulder. There was a resounding *crack!* and the goblin shrieked. Naull whipped her staff around, spinning it in close to her side as she swayed on the big spiderweb. The goblin took one more look at her then turned and ran.

Regdar wasn't sure where it was heading, but he had no time to watch. The krenshar's head appeared over the edge of the pit, and it snarled at him, gobbets of bloody goblin flesh still hanging from its razor-sharp fangs.

Regdar had encountered krenshars before. He knew they had a trick they did to scare their prey stiff. Regdar had seen it work on half a dozen experienced soldiers.

He brought his sword down hard but intentionally slow. The thing had only its front two claws on the step, but it was still able to dodge to the left easily enough. Because Regdar hadn't really been trying to hit it, he was able to get his greatsword back up and in front of his body so that when the krenshar lunged at him, its teeth clanged harmlessly against the flat of his blade. He tried to twist the sword and cut the monster's mouth, but it was quicker than him and managed to get free of it.

The krenshar hopped the rest of the way up out of the pit, and Regdar drew his sword next to his left shoulder—and that's when the thing peeled back its face, revealing bright red muscle, throbbing veins, and horrid, infected black gums. The scream that issued from the thing rattled Regdar's eardrums, and the fighter found the whole thing unsettling. He was supposed to freeze with fear, but he didn't, and he made the krenshar painfully aware of that fact by slashing at it.

The greatsword bit deeply, dragging a deep cut through the matted fur on the monster's chest. Blood poured from the wound, and the timbre of the scream changed enough so that Regdar knew he'd hurt it.

As the krenshar's scream faded and the monster backed off a step, Regdar heard the big hobgoblin barking orders at its goblin warriors.

The krenshar lunged at Regdar, swiping at him with one claw. Regdar slid his foot back, and the claws raked across his jambeau. Regdar let his right wrist go limp so that when the krenshar bit at him, the tip of the sword poked it in the top of its head. The beast was fast enough to drop its head and slide out from under the attack. Regdar made note of the fact that it slid to the left.

The krenshar glanced up at the platform, and Regdar did too. He saw Naull disappear into the tunnel, grabbing the torch as she went. There was a strange sound—stone grinding on stone—that seemed to vibrate up from below. The krenshar noticed it too, and it looked into the pit.

Regdar took that opportunity to kick the creature in the face. It saw the attack coming and dodged to the left—directly into the strong, fast, downward hack of Regdar's greatsword.

The heavy blade split the krenshar's head in two down the middle. Blood sprayed over Regdar and poured onto the smooth stone and over the edge of the pit. He couldn't help following the flow of blood with his eyes, and when he looked down into the pit he saw a second krenshar.

The big hobgoblin was screaming and taking out its frustrations on the goblin who was still being shaken back and forth in its grip. The goblin seemed somehow used to the treatment.

"Death to you, Man!" the hobgoblin screamed. "Death to you!"

The krenshar in the pit screamed in chorus with the hobgoblin, and that seemed to cheer the humanoid up.

"Kill two, Man?" the hobgoblin howled. "I don't think so!"

"What's your name?" Regdar called across the pit as the second krenshar started to make its way up the still unconscious hobgoblin.

The humanoid tipped its head at him and dropped the goblin it had been shaking. The goblin scuttled backward, rejoining the group of goblins and spiders that seemed to be waiting for orders.

The hobgoblin turned to them and growled. The goblins and spiders listened attentively, then all looked at the goblin who had been shaken around. The goblin stood, and Regdar got the feeling it was trying hard not to look at him. It gathered the other four goblins and three of the huge spiders around it, and they started running away, passing through slits in the flowstone wall and into pitch blackness.

The hobgoblin laughed, glanced at the krenshar, and said, "Rezrex. Lord Rezrex."

"Rezrex," Regdar said, also glancing at the approaching krenshar. "I'm Regdar, and I can kill as many as you've got."

If Naull had stopped running and thought about what she was doing, where she was, and where she was going, she might have gone mad. That being the case, she just kept running.

She had a goblin torch in her right hand and her staff in her left hand. The light was bright enough so that if she kept her eyes on the uneven stone floor she could run, though not terribly fast. The tunnel was narrow, and the torch lit the whole thing: walls, ceiling, and floor.

She had gone maybe forty-five or fifty feet down the tunnel when she heard a low, grinding, almost crumbling sound echoing up from the rock beneath her feet. The vibration that accompanied it made butterflies dance in her stomach, but again, she didn't stop to try to find out what it was.

The tunnel made a gradual turn to her right, so she wasn't able to see the goblin she was running after—running after, not *chasing*. She was hoping that after rescuing it from the hobgoblin's bloody fighting pit the goblin might help them find their way out of the caves. The rapid staccato rhythm of the little humanoid's footsteps echoed clearly ahead of her, though, and having come down this tunnel already, she knew she had a decent chance of catching up to it. If she couldn't see the goblin by the time they came out into the larger cave, she doubted she'd ever find it again. Her plan, in that case, would be to go back and hope that Regdar was either close behind her or still alive somewhere back in the goblin community.

She almost lost her footing but managed a more or less controlled slide when the passage sloped steeply downward. She was running again when it leveled off, then it began to slope down again, though this time much more gradually. This helped her to pick up speed. She knew how small the goblin was and could hear by its footsteps that it was running in a flurry of short, fast strides. Naull opened up her own stride, hoping her much longer legs would help her to catch up.

Finally she saw the goblin ahead of her, the stone club gripped in its right hand. It was breathing heavily from the run and was having some trouble making it up a fairly easy slope in the tunnel. Naull, not sure what she would say or do when she did catch up with the goblin, slowed her pace and hung back just enough to keep the humanoid in sight.

The goblin clambered up the spidersilk ladder that led back toward the cages. Naull let it get to the top before she tossed her torch to the floor, tucked her staff through one of her pouch straps, grabbed the ladder, and followed the goblin up.

The torches still burning in the larger cave gave off only a dim, flickering light, but it was enough for Naull to see where she was going. The goblin ran straight for the first cage, maybe thirty feet from where the side-passage emptied out into the larger cave. The goblins inside all cowered back away from the goblin that had come rushing out of the darkness at them, but by the time Naull came out into the area around the cages, she could see them recognize their comrade. They pressed against the stone cage and started clawing at the spidersilk holding the thing shut.

Naull ran for the farther cage—the first one she and Regdar had seen—drawing a crossbow bolt as she did. The caged goblins drew away from her, practically crawling over each other to get as far away from her as possible. Naull tried not to look at them. She didn't like the feeling of anyone being so afraid of her. The little wretches, obviously starved and dying, beaten and desperate, were too sad to look at.

She started to work at the spidersilk with the sharp iron tip of the crossbow bolt when her attention was drawn back to the other cage by some sort of commotion.

The freed goblin was back-stepping and swinging furiously down with its stone club. Naull gasped when she saw the spider charging at the goblin, its sharp mandibles clacking together, the pointed tips of its segmented legs clicking across the cave floor.

Naull grabbed for the crossbow hanging at her back just as the goblin fell. She put the bolt she had in her hand in place on the bow and cocked it while the goblin rolled to one side then the other, trying to avoid the spider's continuous attempts to bite it. When she let fly the bolt, the goblin drew back its club for a blow that Naull was sure would come seconds after the spider had locked its jaws into the little humanoid's neck.

The crossbow bolt drove itself into the spider, ruining at least three of its gleaming black eyes on the way in. The force of it made the quivering, dying creature slide back away from the goblin a good yard or two.

The goblin leaned up, spinning, to look at Naull, its wide mouth open, and its bloodshot eyes bulging in surprise. Naull smiled, not sure what else to do, but the goblin just stared at her. The prisoners were staring too, all in gaping, wide-eyed shock.

Naull grabbed two more crossbow bolts, and the goblin still sitting on the floor threw up its hands, the look of surprise changing immediately to a look of horror. The goblin thought she was going to shoot it, but instead Naull tossed one of the bolts to the humanoid. It clattered to a stop on the floor next to the goblin, and Naull went back to work on the spidersilk with the other. She saw the goblin grab the crossbow bolt and follow suit, to the accompaniment of grunts and squeals from the prisoners.

Soon enough, the spidersilk gave way, and Naull was able to swing open the cage. The goblins inside paused, and Naull looked over at the goblin she'd followed back there. That cage few open as well, and the prisoners inside flooded out. Without a moment's thought or hesitation, the goblin prisoners ran, some stumbling and falling only to be trampled by their comrades in a mass exodus up the gradual incline of the big cave.

Naull was pushed aside by the goblins flooding out of the cage she'd opened. The little cowards fell all over each other to follow their fellows up and out of the deeper cave. Naull had expected them to fight. She had expected . . .

She didn't know.

Regdar was out of time.

Naull had run after the fleeing goblin they'd come to rescue, and the longer she was running away from him, the harder it would be for him to find her—and he had no torch.

The krenshar was out of the pit, staring at Regdar with piercing green eyes brimming with the animalistic hunger of the wild predator. The hobgoblin Rezrex was laughing and barking orders at goblins from across the fighting pit. Regdar knew it was only a matter of time before Rezrex was able to rally his cowardly troops, and Regdar would be overwhelmed by goblins.

An odd mixture of desperation and focus made the muscles in Regdar's huge arms bunch. His fingers cracked as they tightened around the rough leather grip of his heavy greatsword.

The krenshar growled low in that catlike way it had and stepped closer, head low, ready to pounce. Regdar chopped down at the thing, but the krenshar dodged to the left with agility the human couldn't match. The greatsword smashed into the rock floor, sending shards of light brown flowstone spinning through the air all around him. The sound of it echoed loudly for a long time in the huge chamber. The krenshar roared and backed away from the noise, and Regdar could see, from the corner of his eye, Rezrex back away too. The hobgoblin's eyes narrowed, and Regdar was pleased to see the look of fear on the big humanoid's face.

The krenshar, unfortunately, was not quite as put off. The thing snapped at Regdar, turning its head to one side and locking its jaws onto the fighter's right leg, just below his knee.

Regdar grunted when the beast's teeth popped through the steel jambeau and punctured his skin, driving deeply into his rock-hard calf muscle. Reacting as much to the pain as to the threat of any worse injury when the krenshar inevitably began to shake its head and tear his leg apart, Regdar brought his greatsword down in another crushing blow. The krenshar twitched, and Regdar knew it was about to start shaking him. The sword shattered the krenshar's spine as it passed almost halfway through the creature's lithe, catlike body.

The jaws came off Regdar's leg so fast and so hard—part of violent spasms that rippled through the monster's fast-dying body—that several fangs were left behind, hanging in the ragged holes in Regdar's armor.

Regdar roared in pain and relief and stepped forward next to the dead krenshar, keeping as much weight on his left leg as he could. He could feel his wounded right leg stiffening up, and when he saw the hobgoblin withdrawing into the darkness behind the flowstone curtain, Regdar gave up the thought of confronting Rezrex.

Limping, he made his way to the spidersilk ladder that ran up to the platform and the side-passage beyond. It wasn't easy negotiating the spidersilk, but he finally rolled onto the platform and struggled to his feet.

He took only two steps into the dark tunnel when his leg collapsed. Gritting his teeth to hold back a scream, Regdar knew he would have to tend to his wounds—and light a torch—before he could follow Naull. He only hoped she was alive and bringing the other goblin prisoners back with her to help.

Naull wasn't sure if she should help the goblin open the third cage or not, so she stood back, near one rough stone wall, and watched. It took the goblin a few long minutes to saw through the spidersilk, breaking the crossbow bolt in the process, but the last group of prisoners were freed in due course.

The goblin shouted at them in their primitive tongue, tried to grab them as they rushed past him, but they didn't hesitate to follow their comrades up the cave and away. Some of them spared their savior a glance, some even, in Naull's estimation, looked guilty for not stopping, but every last one of them ran for it.

The goblin stomped his feet, spittle shooting from his frustrated grimace. Naull stepped a few strides toward him and said, "It's all right."

The goblin stopped and looked up at her, and Naull forced a smile.

"Do you understand me?" she asked, the cascade of echoes that followed making it hard for her to even understand herself.

The goblin looked at her vacantly, making it plain that he didn't understand her. He did look like he was about to speak, though, when the unmistakable sound of running feet echoed up the huge cave. Naull was no expert, but even she knew that there was a group, maybe a big group, of goblins on their way, and on their way fast.

About thirty feet into the narrow tunnel, the passage widened on one side to form a sort of niche. Regdar had to feel his way along the wall with his right hand until he found the space and managed to duck inside, scraping the top of his already battered helm along the low ceiling.

Working to get his breathing under control, Regdar fished in his backpack, and found a torch and his flint and steel. When he had the torch lit, he stopped, his greatsword in his right hand, and listened. There were sounds echoing in the cool air around him, but the sounds were all coming from far away. He didn't think any of the goblins had braved the narrow confines of the passage to come after him.

Hoping that would hold true for a while longer—and likewise hoping that Naull was safe wherever she was—he pulled off the fang-punctured jambeau from his right leg. The armor piece came off his calf, and the few fangs the krenshar left behind clattered to the stone floor.

Regdar set his jaw against the pain and examined the wounds. They weren't too deep, but they were bleeding freely. He pulled an old sack out of his backpack and tore it into strips. It wasn't the best material—or the cleanest—for bandages, but it would have to do.

He wrapped his calf, but not too tight, then unstrapped the cuisse from the front of his right thigh. The dagger wound was worse—both bigger and deeper—and Regdar used all the rest of the sack tying the wound closed. It continued to seep blood, and Regdar knew he would have to find Jozan if he had any hope of it healing properly.

Knowing he wouldn't find Jozan—or Naull—sitting in the little niche, Regdar put the damaged armor pieces back into place, took up his torch, and stood. The pain was bearable, and, limping, Regdar set off down the narrow passage.

Naull looked around, unsure what to do, then looked at the goblin. The little humanoid was looking around quickly as well, but when their eyes met, he grunted at her in a way that made Naull think he was speaking to her, then he slid into the still water of the little pool next to the cage.

The sight gave Naull a chill, and she shivered in the cool subterranean air, but she got the message: *hide.*

She had no intention of getting wet again, and there was the narrow passage she and Regdar had passed through when they'd first discovered the cages. It was a dark, confined space, and she backed into it quickly until she was cloaked in inky darkness.

She could see five goblins—all armed—accompanied by three of the huge brown spiders. She couldn't help thinking she recognized one of the goblins.

The party paused in front of the cages, barking guttural grunts at each other, then they continued on, chasing the freed prisoners up the wide cave. Naull waited until their footsteps were barely audible echoes before she slipped out of the darkness.

The goblin came up out of the water, shivering and looking even more wretched and desperate than before. He looked at her, obviously waiting for Naull to make the first move.

In response, the young mage held both of her hands, palm out, and said, "It's all right. I won't hurt you."

She felt ridiculous for even speaking to a goblin whom she knew didn't understand the Common Tongue, but she didn't know what else to do. Strangely enough, the goblin tilted his head at her, almost seeming to understand. The gesture must have been just universal enough to assuage his fears.

Naull held her hand in front of her and tried to make the shape of Regdar in the air.

"The big guy," she said. "My friend? The big human guy with the giant sword?"

She pointed down the cave in the direction of the goblin community, the fighting pit, and Regdar. The goblin glanced back in the direction she indicated then grunted at her in a questioning manner.

Naull stepped forward, trotting past him pumping her arms to indicate that they should run. She felt like a fool, but again, the goblin seemed to get the message. He let loose a long string of grunts, waving his arms in front of him in some odd pantomime that Naull couldn't figure out at all.

"Come on," she said, moving into the darkness.

The goblin grabbed the torch that was stuck in the wall next to the pool, and when Naull started running down the middle of the descending cave floor, he followed alongside her with grim determination.

They might have gone forty yards—passing two more little pools and the pitch-black entrance to a side-passage that made Naull feel strangely uneasy—when the goblin stopped.

The cave narrowed dramatically to less than ten feet, and as they passed through, a huge, hairy, gray-skinned arm reached out from behind a curve in the rock wall and smashed into the goblin's chest. Naull skidded to a halt, almost losing her footing, just as the big hobgoblin stepped out in front of her, a remarkably well-crafted mace in one hand and her goblin companion in the other.

He smiled at her in a way that made Naull want to scream.

"I don't think they climbed down there," Lidda said, standing at the edge of a sheer ten-foot drop on one side of the enormous cave. "Naull isn't really a climber, and Redguy seems to take a more direct approach."

Jozan sighed, peering into the darkness beyond the edge of Lidda's lanternlight. There was a narrow opening to what looked like some sort of side-passage at the bottom of the depression. Regdar and Naull could easily have fit through, but Jozan thought Lidda was probably correct in her assumption that—

"Jump!" Lidda stage-whispered.

Jozan surprised himself by actually jumping off the edge. He hit the stone floor hard but managed a roll that surprised him more than the fact that he jumped. He scrambled to his feet, unhurt.

He had heard the sudden cacophony of echoing footsteps increasing in volume and intensity. It was obvious that whatever was coming was coming toward them. Jozan knew that his first reaction wouldn't have been to jump off the edge and hide while whatever it was ran past. He felt embarrassed and more than a little angry.

"Lidda," he hissed, looking up.

The halfling was hanging by her fingertips from the sharp edge of the drop-off. The distance between her feet and the floor was easily as tall as Jozan, if not a few inches taller.

Lidda turned her head enough to see him and winked. "I didn't mean all the way. . . ." she whispered.

Jozan opened his mouth to chastise her when the footsteps, mixed with guttural grunts and barks the priest recognized as goblin speech, moved past them.

Lidda bent her arms, lifting herself up just enough to peek over the edge, and Jozan moved as quickly and as quietly as he could to press his back against the wall. He could see Lidda's head turn from the direction they had been headed, back to the direction of the waterfalls. She was obviously following a group of running goblins.

When the sound started to fade again into muddier echoes, Lidda looked down and said, "They looked scared."

Jozan scanned the wall for any kind of hand- or toe-hold and found one he thought would help him boost himself up to the edge. His mind raced through the many things he wanted to yell at Lidda for.

"Two-to-one says Riptare's down that way," the halfling said, looking off in the direction the running goblins had come from.

The longer Regdar walked and the faster he pushed himself, the more his right leg actually loosened up. He heard and saw no sign of Naull or the goblin until he came up under the sinkhole that they'd climbed down from the cages.

A torch was laying on the floor, its flame reduced to a trace of orange glowing around the black stub. The thing had left a trail of scorched rock, and it looked to Regdar as if the torch had rolled from its original position. When he realized where the thing had rolled to, he hissed a sharp curse.

The torch had rolled into the spidersilk ladder. All that was left of the ladder was a length of the creamy white rope hanging a good two feet out of Regdar's reach. The floor below it was littered with ash. The light from Regdar's torch barely reached the rim of the sinkhole.

He scanned around him, but there was no way to climb it—not fast, and not in armor.

That's when he heard the scream.

"Naull," he said aloud, then cursed the burned ladder again.

He was sure it was the young mage who'd screamed, but the only choice he had was to go deeper down the narrow passage and hope it came out someplace he might recognize—someplace close to Naull.

Jozan was just pushing himself over the edge of the drop-off when the shrill scream echoed through the air around him. Startled, he almost lost his grip and fell back down into the depression.

"That was Naull," Lidda said, concern creasing her grimy face.

Jozan wanted to tell her that she couldn't be sure, that it might be a goblin, or anyone else but Naull, but he couldn't.

He climbed up and got to his feet. Lidda skipped past him, then stopped a couple yards away, in the center of the big cave.

"Can you tell which way it was coming from?" the priest asked.

The halfling had her head cocked to one side, obviously listening, and she held up a finger.

Jozan had to work hard to remain silent, but he managed it.

"I think . . ." the halfling finally whispered. "I think . . ."

She glanced at the mouth of another side-passage on the other side of the cave, then back down the wider main tunnel.

"Naull?" she called into the darkness.

Jozan heard footsteps approaching, but with the echoes he couldn't tell how many, how big, or even what was approaching. Either way, Naull didn't answer. He hefted his mace and set his feet apart—

—and a goblin brushed right past him, yelping, obviously as surprised to see the priest as the priest was to see it.

Tzrg was so used to being scared that when he practically ran into the human, he wasn't as terrified as he would normally have been, he was just sort of startled. For a moment, the goblin thought it was the same huge, armored human who had killed Rezrex's pet *ksr*, but as Tzrg slid to a stop he saw the human's mace, remembered that the other one had a really big sword, and knew that this was a different human.

Tzrg had never seen a human in his life, now there were two in one day. He couldn't imagine that they were friends of the Cavemouth Tribe but if not, why would they be down there?

Maybe Rezrex had some old enemies. Tzrg had no trouble believing that.

The human brought his mace down toward Tzrg, who put his own sword up in front of his forehead to parry the blow. The mace banged into his sword with enough force to bend the rusty old blade almost in half. Tzrg's arm followed the blow down and spun around out of control, almost hard enough to dislocate his shoulder.

Tzrg stepped back, holding in a scream so that Pwmk—one of his few remaining sergeants—and the less capable warriors Pvpj, Lkrt, and Kspf wouldn't see him further humiliate himself.

The fact that Pwmk was with him, chasing down the freed Cavemouth prisoners, was a small consolation. Pwmk could fight and usually didn't run away unless he got hurt. The other three, especially Lkrt, were undisciplined cowards—goblins after Tzrg's own heart.

It didn't surprise Tzrg to see Lkrt running right past the human, continuing on his way in the wake of the fleeing prisoners, but he was surprised to see the female. She looked like a human, but was much shorter—goblin sized—but ugly: smooth and kind of pink, with weird hair and tiny, unsettlingly alert eyes. She had a lantern, and Tzrg cursed his rash inattention at not having noticed that they were running into light past where they usually maintained torches.

Pwmk and Pvpj ran up to the female, obviously making to grab her, expecting no resistance. Tzrg hoped this little human was as timid as a goblin female. One of the hive spiders was on the floor in back of them, another on the wall behind them and to their left, and the third scuttled up next to Kspf, who was, as usual, taking up the rear.

The armored human said something in their impossibly complex, sing-songy tongue and swung his mace at Tzrg again. This time, Tzrg ducked and stabbed at the human from under his guard.

If his sword wasn't bent in half, it might have had a chance of scratching the man's armor, but instead it slid across the human's steel-encased thigh with a painfully shrill screech of metal on metal.

From between the human's legs, Tzrg could see the female kick Pvpj in the danglies—hard enough to drop him. Pwmk stabbed at her with his javelin, but Tzrg didn't see if he managed to run her through or not. The armored human swiped across with the heavy mace in a backhanded attack Tzrg never saw coming. The giant weapon punched into his chest, driving the air from the goblin's lungs. Tzrg tried to take a breath, but couldn't. He took two steps backward, wondering what was causing all the flashing lights, then he blinked and felt as if the world was spinning around and around. He heard a high-pitched scream, thought it might be him screaming, then fell facefirst to the hard, cold stone floor of the cave, all the while hoping he would be dead soon.

Regdar heard a woman scream, "*Ow!*" but in the confines of the narrow side-passage it sounded more like: "*Ow-ow-ow-ow-ow-ow-ow-ow-ow . . .*"

When that was followed by "You son of a *bitch!*" he knew it was Lidda, and he ran faster.

The tunnel ended all at once, and he came out into a wider space with a much higher ceiling—one well out of the edge of his torchlight. In front of him was a flat stone wall, and Regdar barely managed to skip to a stop—his wounded right leg protesting the maneuver with jolts of wicked pain—in time to keep from crashing into it.

Something about the wall seemed familiar, and all at once he remembered passing the steep depression in the side of the cave, not long after he and Naull had come out of the waterfalls and before they found the caged goblins.

Regdar looked up and saw Jozan standing on the edge of the drop-off above him. He heard the sounds of someone fighting, but couldn't see Lidda. Jozan, who didn't see Regdar, moved away from the edge with a purpose to his stride. Regdar could hear his loud, clanging footsteps recede at a run, then a goblin grunted and more sounds of battle echoed in the cave.

Regdar found a convenient toe-hold in the wall and, still holding his greatsword in his right hand, boosted up enough to grab the edge with his left hand.

He heard Lidda grunting and growling like a goblin, and there was the unmistakable *tap-tap-tap* of one or more of the spiders echoing through the cave as well. Regdar lifted himself up with a grunt and rolled over the edge, brushing past the fallen form of a goblin that was laying on its back, wheezing, its eyes rolled up into its skull.

Lidda was standing over another fallen goblin, this one rolling on the cave floor with its hands clutched between its legs. She'd taken a nasty cut on her right shoulder, and the blood on the tip of the javelin of the goblin facing her made the source of the wound obvious. She was batting the javelin away with her short sword, but this goblin had a fierce, almost confident look in its eyes, and Regdar was worried for the halfling.

Jozan, meanwhile, was making fast work of another goblin on the other side of the cave, at the far edge of Lidda's lanternlight. That goblin looked more concerned with escape than fighting back, and Jozan took it down fast enough.

Regdar ran toward Lidda, purposely not saying anything for fear he would startle her into letting her guard down. She parried another jab from the goblin's javelin, then another goblin, with a spider on each side of it, moved up toward her.

Regdar kept running and blew past Lidda close enough that her long braid whipped against his armor. The goblin who had cut her looked up only a second before Regdar ran it right over. The fighter stumbled as he trampled the goblin. He heard bones crack, and knew they were the goblin's bones. To keep from injuring himself he had to fall into a roll.

The goblin who had been coming up behind squealed and jumped away, almost tripping over its friend that was still more concerned with the pain between its legs.

Regdar rolled onto his back and threw out his left arm to stop himself.

"*Regdar!*" Lidda squealed, obviously happy enough, or surprised enough, to use his real name.

He was about to chide her for that when something fell on his head. Sharp, pointed things scratched at his face, and he realized it was one of the spiders. He grabbed it with his left hand and saw the thing's hideous mouth only inches from his face—then the tip of a steel blade even closer. He threw his head back to avoid being skewered in the eye and threw the spider off him.

"Careful," he growled when he scrambled to his feet and saw Lidda stepping on the spider's back, trying to pull her sword out of the thing's twitching body.

"You're welcome, Ratmor," she said with a smile, and her blade came free.

Ignoring her, Regdar turned to the last standing goblin. He had to run several fast steps to catch up to the fleeing humanoid, but when he did, Regdar grabbed the goblin by its loose, ragged shirt, and smashed its face into the cave wall. Blood and teeth marked the impact, and the goblin went limp.

"Regdar," Jozan said from behind him, "where's Naull?"

17

If **Naull didn't need** the contents of her pouches so badly, she might have tried to wriggle free of the straps to get away. The huge hobgoblin was holding her up off the floor, its strong hand wrapped around one of the wide leather straps. She felt like a doll being dragged along by a spoiled, careless child. The goblin she was beginning to think of as a friend was in no better shape. The hobgoblin's other hand was closed around the goblin's arm tight enough that Naull could see the goblin's hand going pale.

Her voice scratchy and hoarse from the scream, Naull said, "Let me go. . . ."

The hobgoblin laughed—an evil, unpleasant sound—and said, "Rezrex give orders, female."

The thing barked a string of grunts at the goblin, who seemed to understand. The smaller humanoid snarled and turned to look at the floor, where its stone club was slowly rolling away.

"You speak . . ." Naull said, huffing as she was swung back and forth and her legs scraped on the floor, ". . . Common. You speak Common."

Rezrex was striding confidently back in the direction from which Naull and her new friend had come. Strange noises continued to echo around her, and even if she wasn't disoriented from being half-dragged, half-carried, she wouldn't have been able to sort out the sounds. She imagined she heard voices—Lidda, Jozan, even Regdar—but chalked it up to wishful thinking.

"Why are you doing this?" she asked, referring to her own capture at first but realizing quickly enough that she didn't understand any of what was happening.

The hobgoblin was obviously in control of the goblins who lived deeper in the caves, below the waterfalls. And the goblins—or the hobgoblins—were in control of the spiders. There was another tribe that lived closer to the surface, and they had been captured by the hobgoblin's tribe.

"Are you sending the spiders to attack the herds?" she asked.

The hobgoblin stopped and lifted her up to regard her coolly. Naull got her feet under her and stood, taking some of the weight off the strap that was biting into her shoulder. The hobgoblin lifted her an inch off the ground in response—Naull wasn't that heavy after all—and scowled into her face.

"Herds?" Rezrex asked. "Spiders above gone wild. Rezrex not care what they do. Rezrex bring tribes together."

"Let me go," she said.

The hobgoblin coughed out a laugh, spraying her with vile-smelling spittle that caused her to gag.

There was some commotion, and Naull saw a hand wrap itself around the hilt of the hobgoblin's jagged-edged dagger. The weapon was hanging from the hobgoblin's belt, next to the dangling mace. At first, Naull thought she was dead, then she realized that the hand was too small to be Rezrex's.

The goblin drew the heavy dagger from the hobgoblin's sheath and in the process dragged it across the big humanoid's waist, opening a nasty cut.

The hobgoblin roared and tossed Naull to the side. She fell, her arms flapping wildly at her side, and hit the floor hard. Her teeth smashed together painfully, and she hoped she hadn't broken any of them. She was sure she'd have a bruise on her backside for weeks to come—if she lived that long.

As she crab-walked away from the hobgoblin, she watch Rezrex smash the goblin into the floor hard enough to knock the dagger from his hand. The weapon clattered away in the opposite direction, and Naull cursed her misfortune.

At the same time the goblin lost its hold on the dagger, though, Rezrex lost his hold on the goblin. The smaller humanoid leaped to its feet, obviously in pain but desperate to get out of the hobgoblin's reach.

Rezrex grabbed for his mace as Naull dug into one of her pouches. The hobgoblin took a hard swipe at the goblin, who managed to roll out of the way. Naull began to speak the words of her spell as quietly as she could. The goblin tried to make for the dagger, but Rezrex cut him off with a downward thrust of the mace that cracked the stone floor between the goblin and the dagger.

Naull's fingers came out of her pouch with a dead firefly pinched between them, and Rezrex obviously heard her chanting.

The hobgoblin spun around and yelled, "Silence, witch!"

He held his mace above his head and stepped toward her. Fear almost made her fumble the last few syllables of the spell, but she finished it and slapped her hand across the beast's face.

Bright yellow light blazed from the hobgoblin's face, and Naull pumped her fist once and breathed, "Yes!"

The hobgoblin clasped his free hand over his face, and Naull could see the magic light shine between his huge, gnarled fingers.

Rezrex roared and stepped back, almost stepping on the goblin's hand. The goblin, who was reaching for the dagger, decided against another attempt. Without sparing Naull a glance, the goblin got to his feet and ran.

Naull couldn't stop herself from yelling, "Hey!" at the goblin's receding back.

Rezrex, still growling, blind, responded to her voice, turning on her. Naull got to her feet, but the hobgoblin came at her. He swiped blindly with his mace and came within an inch of smashing Naull's skull.

She yelped, and the hobgoblin took his hands away from his face. Light blazed out from the hobgoblin's eyes, and Naull, her own eyes having grown accustomed to the dim lighting, found herself cringing away from the blinding magical luminescence.

Rezrex grabbed at her, and she tried to bat his arm away with her own hand. All that succeeded in doing was giving Rezrex a better indication of where she was. His hand closed around her waist with a crushing, bruising force.

She had to close her eyes—the light from Rezrex's eyes was so bright—but she could feel the hobgoblin dragging her up the cave.

"Goblins will come together as one under Rezrex," the blinded hobgoblin bellowed. "I start clearing out humans next!"

"I recognize this one," Regdar said, standing over the first goblin Jozan had taken down.

Regdar was certain it was the goblin who had been shaken around by Rezrex, then sent away with—Regdar looked at the scattered bodies—exactly this group of goblins and spiders.

Jozan, who was finishing off the last of the three spiders, looked up and asked, "Is he their leader?"

Regdar shook his head, looking down at the unconscious goblin as Jozan and Lidda came to stand next to him. "Their leader is a hobgoblin—much bigger, meaner—named Rezrex."

"You're wounded," the priest said.

"I know," Lidda answered, "and it hurts like a son of a—"

"I was talking to Regdar," Jozan answered.

The coldness in his voice made Regdar turn around. The priest stood behind him, facing the halfling, who was looking up at him with that expression Regdar had seen on a hundred faces—just before a tavern brawl broke out.

"Nice," the halfling said. "I wonder if Pelor will be able to get my foot out of your—"

"Naull might be dying out there somewhere," Regdar interjected.

Jozan and Lidda both looked at him, and their faces softened simultaneously.

"This might not be the chief," Regdar continued, gesturing at the unconscious goblin, "but I think he might be some kind of lieutenant."

Jozan considered the goblin and said, "Can you talk to him?"

Regdar was about to tell him no, when he realized the priest was talking to Lidda.

The halfling stepped closer to the goblin and said, "Sure, if we can wake him up."

Regdar unslung his backpack and took out his waterskin.

"Ask him where Naull is," Jozan suggested.

Lidda and Jozan stepped back, and Regdar started to pour water over the goblin's face.

Tzrg, certain his wretched soul had been sent to the Hell of Having Water Splashed in Your Face, sputtered and coughed, and tried to remember any kind of prayer he could use to impress Maglubiyet enough to keep the demon god of goblins from eating him alive.

He couldn't think of one, but he did manage to catch his breath and open his eyes.

Tzrg didn't know whether to be happy or disappointed to see that he wasn't dead. Maglubiyet wasn't going to eat him alive, but the three bizarre humans—two big armored males and the little female—who were standing over him might do something even worse.

He wanted more than anything to get up and run away, but he recognized one of the humans as the man who'd killed a hobgoblin, two krenshars, and a handful of hive spiders. The other male was the one who had knocked him out—damn near killed him—with a mace as long as Tzrg was tall. He looked at the female and instinctively put a hand over his crotch.

The human who had knocked him out looked at the female and spoke in their impossible-to-fathom language then turned to the other man and spoke some more. The human with the mace took a shield from his back and handed it to the other man, who took it with a smile.

The female leaned over him and cleared her throat. Tzrg winced at the sound. His chest hurt, his head hurt, and he was getting sick of being held prisoner by tall things with armor and maces. He hoped that they would decide to let the bigger human kill him. The giant sword should make fast work of a little goblin.

They didn't kill him, though—at least not right away. The female looked down at him and said something, followed by what Tzrg was sure was the Goblin word for "name."

She pointed at him and repeated herself, then said, "*Gbn rblmg.*"

She wanted him to speak. Her accent was weird—stranger even that Rezrex's—but she was making sense, though he still wasn't sure what she wanted him to say.

He opened his mouth to say something—anything—but his chest hurt too much. One of the humans reached down for him, and Tzrg wished he was able to move, so he could roll out of the way, then he decided to let them kill him.

All the human did, though, was sit him up. His chest still hurt, but a lot of the pressure was gone, and he could breathe better.

The female said, "Lidda *kgl*." Her name was Lidda.

It was as hard to say as Rezrex, but it was a name—at least he thought it was. She wanted to know what his name was.

"*Tzrg*," he said, looking up at her and hoping that the look in his eyes would inspire them to kill him quickly.

The female smiled, and Tzrg had no idea how to take that. The other two humans didn't seem to understand.

"Lidda *bkn*," she said. "*Bkn* Lidda. *Pmldl* Tzrg."

She wanted a foreigner that belonged to her, and she wanted Tzrg to get it.

The female waved her arms at her sides and wiggled her fingers in a way that made Tzrg think of spiders, then she made curvy gestures with both hands like a female—a female spider. She wanted the Cavemouth Tribe's hive spider queen.

Tzrg couldn't begin to guess why, but at least he knew where that was, and it wasn't even far away. If that's all they wanted, they could have it. Of course, if they made off with the Cavemouth Tribe's hive spider queen, Rezrex would be angry and probably . . .

Tzrg decided not to think about that and started the painful process of climbing to his feet—only flinching a little when the human with the mace took his arm to help him—realizing that he would just have to go with whatever the big, mace-wielding outsiders who were closest by wanted him to do, and the humans were closer than Rezrex.

He wanted them to know he would do as they asked and that

they should follow him, so he looked at the female and said, "*Bkn gnrbt. Tzrg pzvmp.*"

Regdar's skin was crawling. He wanted to run blindly down the length of the cave in search of Naull. He wanted to do just about anything but trust a goblin to bring them to her.

"You're sure . . ." he said to Lidda, who was following closely behind the goblin, grunting at it.

The halfling sighed and said, "I want to find her as much as you do, Redjar. Unless you have some bright idea, we follow Tzrg."

"Tzrg?" Jozan asked. The priest didn't look any more confident than Regdar.

"That's his name," Lidda replied. "He was the chief of the Stonedeep Tribe before the hobgoblin Rezrex showed up and took over. They raided the Cavemouth Tribe, who live farther up near the surface, and kidnapped their mother or something . . . whatever that means. That caused some kind of problem, and they managed to capture most of the Cavemouth goblins and hold them prisoner. Rezrex wants to unite the tribes and be . . . I don't know what. . . . King of the Goblins or something?"

They walked quickly behind the scurrying goblin who kept glancing over his shoulder as if afraid that one or all three of them were going to stab him in the back. He was leading them toward the dark mouth of one of the nearby side-passages.

"You got all that from grunting at this goblin?" Regdar said, unable to believe it.

Lidda didn't look back at him when she said, "Humans. Like it would kill you to learn a foreign language."

18

Only maybe half a dozen yards down the narrow side-passage, their way was blocked by stalactites and stalagmites tied together with spidersilk and fashioned into bars. Regdar made sure he stood in the middle of the passage at the back of the party in case their goblin prisoner decided to turn tail and make a run for it.

Lidda kept up her grunting conversation with the little humanoid, and when she stopped at the bars, she turned to Regdar and Jozan and said, "I think she's in there."

Regdar, his greatsword in his right hand and shield in his left, shifted his feet and tried to keep his blood from boiling.

"It can't be," he said.

Jozan turned to him with a questioning look.

"She was ahead of me," Regdar said. "She was free and clear. All the goblins were behind her, and the only group of them that ran up this way were this little guy and his friends. There wasn't anyone to capture her and put her in a cage."

Lidda opened her mouth to argue, then obviously thought against it. She turned on the goblin with an irritated scowl. When she grunted at him, the goblin's response was a string of guttural gibberish, but his manner was groveling and apologetic.

A sound echoed from the pitch darkness behind the bars, and Regdar stepped forward.

"Naull?" he called.

The only reply was another echoing sound like a heavy weight shifting against loose stones.

"Who's in there?" Jozan asked Lidda.

The halfling held up her lantern, hesitantly reaching between the crude stone bars. Jozan stepped closer behind her, and so did Regdar, but the big fighter made sure he was all but pressing the cowering goblin into the bars.

Regdar squinted into the darkness and saw something moving just at the edge of Lidda's lanternlight.

"What is that?" he asked.

"I don't know," Lidda said, backing away a little, "but it ain't Naull."

The goblin barked at her, and Lidda turned on him sharply, then backed even farther away from the bars.

Jozan asked, "What did he say?"

"It's a spider," the halfling replied.

As if in reply, the thing behind the bars drew itself slowly into the pool of light from Lidda's lantern. It was the same dull, pale beige color as the spiders they'd encountered before, but bigger—much bigger. Regdar felt the hair on the back of his neck rise. The creature pulled itself out of the darkness as if it was crawling from the womb, revealing two chitinous, segmented legs, then two more, then two more, and two more. Its body was bulbous, an irregular oval shape covered in coarse fur. The front of it was a mass of irregularly spaced jet black eyes. Its mouth was small, with fangs smaller than its cousins. It was impossible for Regdar to tell which of the four of them the creature was looking at—it might have been looking at all of them at once.

"It's the mother," Lidda said.

Jozan gave her a curious look, then his eyes widened as some idea seemed to dawn on him all at once.

"A queen," he said. "It's a hive queen, like a queen bee or a queen ant. The spiders we've fought must be workers . . . drones."

"They hold the queen prisoner," Lidda said, "and use her to control the spiders."

"Extraordinary," Jozan whispered.

Regdar felt his jaw tighten and said, "Should I kill it?"

Jozan was about to answer when they all heard the footsteps echo around them. Regdar was the first to react, pressing against the cave wall and using the back of his right hand to shove the goblin along with him.

He was gratified to see Jozan and Lidda follow his lead and press their backs against the opposite wall. Lidda drew the hood of her lantern down, dimming the light.

The footsteps grew closer and closer.

Naull was struggling just to breathe. Rezrex was holding her around the waist and squeezing. It was still hard for her to see where he was carrying her, dragging her feet behind them. Blind, the hobgoblin moved slowly, hesitantly, shouting orders in its own primitive language as it went. Sounds echoed all around her, and she couldn't tell where they were coming from or what they were. All that mixed with the pungent, horrid odor of the hobgoblin, making Naull's head spin, so she had to fight every second just to stay conscious.

She felt a hand on her—rough and forceful—and heard another voice. She opened her eyes and turned her head, silently cursing at the pain—and at the hobgoblin. There was another of the big humanoids that Naull could see, and she was sure she could hear a third hobgoblin approaching from behind them. They spoke to each other in urgent tones—like soldiers—that reminded her of Regdar.

"Regdar," she tried to scream but managed only a pained squeak, "Regdar . . . help me . . ."

"Regdar?" Rezrex growled.

The hobgoblin grunted an order at one of his lieutenants, and Naull felt a strong hand wrap around first one wrist then the other. Rezrex let go of her waist, and she fell from his grip, only to be pulled back by the other hobgoblin. She could see Rezrex facing her, one hand clamped over his still blazing eyes. The hobgoblin that held her twisted one of her arms painfully behind her and blew hot, rancid breath on her neck.

"Regdar?" Rezrex said again. "I kill that man."

"No," Naull said, squinting at him, trying not to throw up.

She tried to bring to mind a spell but couldn't. She'd cast as many spells as she could in one day. She wasn't sure what happened to her staff and couldn't get to her crossbow with her hands held behind her. She was at the hobgoblin's mercy, and for the first time since walking out of Larktiss Dathiendt's tower, she wanted to go home.

"You his female?" Rezrex asked, his face twisted in pain and anger.

Naull said nothing.

"Not anymore," the hobgoblin sneered, and the one holding her wrists began to laugh.

The sound made Naull's skin crawl.

Rezrex stepped back, saying something to the third hobgoblin. That one stepped forward and drew his arm back, his big hand clenched into a fist. As the hobgoblin's knuckles rushed toward her face, Naull had just enough time to think, That's going to hurt, before finding out how right she was.

She could feel blood gush from her nose, her eyes closed tightly all on their own, and she was out.

Regdar could see by the dim silhouette in the sparse light of Lidda's lantern that it was a goblin. The humanoid ran into the cave and slid to a halt, turning and putting up its hands in a way that indicated to Regdar that the goblin had seen one, some, or all of them.

Without pause, Regdar kicked at the goblin's feet just as Lidda opened the hood of her lantern, filling the little cave with light.

The goblin, eyes wide, mouth open, hopped up over Regdar's sweeping leg, shifted in the air, and came down in an attempt to stomp on Regdar's calf. Though he doubted the little humanoid could put enough weight into the stomp to break his leg, Regdar reacted quickly and rolled with the momentum of his kick. The goblin came down way off the mark, stomping only onto the unforgiving rock floor. The jolt almost knocked it over, unbalancing it enough so that it couldn't dodge or deflect Jozan's mace, which punched into its right side hard enough to drive air from its lungs and drop it to its left knee.

Regdar continued his roll, changing direction, and smashed the goblin with his shield. The goblin fell backward, and Jozan caught it around the waist.

As Regdar leaped to his feet, the goblin Lidda called Tzrg started to move behind him. Regdar had intended to drop his shield and grab the goblin Jozan was holding, but when he saw the other goblin trying to make a break for it, he drew up short and shot his right elbow back. Tzrg didn't even see it coming. Regdar's elbow smashed him into the cave wall, and Tzrg tripped, sprawling onto the floor behind the big human.

The goblin Jozan was holding shook his head once and stood, slipping out of the priest's tenuous, surprised grip. Regdar stepped in front of the goblin and whipped his sword in a half-arc fast enough to make it whistle through the air. The newcomer skidded to a stop with the tip of Regdar's blade less than an inch from the end of its wide, flat nose.

Lidda said something in the goblin language as Jozan brushed past behind Regdar to help Tzrg to his feet and detain him at the same time. Regdar finally had a chance to see the newcomer's face clearly, and he recognized the goblin at once.

"This is the one we saved from the krenshar pit," Regdar said. "Naull went after him."

Lidda spoke to the goblin, a look of stern determination on her face. Waiting for the grunting exchange to yield anything understandable was like torture for Regdar. He stopped short of trying to imagine what might be happening—or what might have happened—to Naull. He could feel his teeth grinding.

The huge, misshapen hive spider queen rubbed its bulbous form against the stone bars. The sound made all of them look in its direction. The creature tapped its needle-pointed legs against the stone and waved its hideous, asymmetrical head from side to side.

The goblin looked at the monster spider with an oddly soft expression Regdar associated with the way some people look at their horses or their dogs.

"The spider . . ." Regdar started to say.

"The queen recognizes this one as a member of the Cavemouth Tribe," Jozan said. "When they brought it down here it must have lost contact with its drones. The drones went wild . . ."

"And attacked the sheep," Regdar finished for him.

"It's what caused all this chaos in the first place," Jozan said. "Lidda . . . ?"

The halfling stopped her grunting speech and looked up at Jozan.

"Is this goblin from the Cavemouth Tribe?" the priest asked.

"He is," Lidda answered. "I think he might be Klnk's son."

Jozan drew in a breath and stood straighter, pulling the goblin Tzrg up with him. The prisoner whimpered and kept his eyes on the floor.

"He *is* Klnk's son," Lidda said, her eyes searching Jozan's face for some idea what to do next.

"Who's son?" asked Regdar.

"Klnk," Jozan answered, pronouncing the goblin name with some difficulty. "He was the chief of the Cavemouth Tribe. He's dead."

Regdar watched Lidda tell the goblin that his father was dead. The goblin sagged visibly.

"I assume that makes him chief now," Regdar said. "We saved him from the krenshar pit. If he wants to return the favor . . ."

"Tell him we can help him," the priest said. "Tell him that if he can keep the spiders in the cave, away from the village and the herds, that we'll help him regain his tribe and get rid of the hobgoblin."

Lidda nodded and started speaking Goblin again. The prisoner looked suspicious, unsure.

"Ask him about Naull," Regdar said. "She was following him."

Lidda nodded and started grunting at the goblin, who answered back quickly, making gestures that Regdar found disturbing.

"Rezrex has her," Lidda said.

Regdar felt the blood drain from his face.

"The hobgoblin?" Jozan asked, his voice quiet and heavy.

Regdar nodded.

"He said he'd help us," Lidda said, glancing between Regdar and

Jozan. "I'm not a hundred percent sure we can trust him, but we might not have much choice. He wants us to release the . . . the queen."

The goblin Tzrg ventured a series of tentative grunts Lidda's way, and whatever he said made the halfling smile.

"They both want Rezrex dead," Lidda told them. "Tzrg wants things to go back the way they were."

Regdar saw the two goblins exchange a look he'd seen a few times in the past. Enemies had turned into allies in more ways than one.

19

Jozan ran after Lidda and the goblin named Glnk, knowing more than usual that his life was in the hands of Pelor. The goblins so far had proved alternately aggressive and cowardly, malign and pitiful, cunning and stupid. Lidda was the only one who could talk to them, and the apparent misunderstanding that had caused Tzrg to bring them to the hive spider queen instead of Naull shook Jozan's confidence in her language skills.

It might be true that the common enemy of both of the goblin tribes and their human neighbors was the hobgoblin Rezrex, but Jozan had to admit, at least to himself, that he didn't have any idea whether or not either Glnk or Tzrg were serious about standing up against the hobgoblin—something neither had been successful at before. The goblins were certainly more closely related to the hobgoblin on most every level than they were to three humans and a halfling. He just had to hope that the goblins believed they would return to the surface after Rezrex was dealt with and the spiders were brought back under control. It was the truth, after all, but who could guess what a goblin was thinking?

The hideous, bloated form of the hive spider queen ambled along next to him, making Jozan even less comfortable.

He recited a silent prayer to Pelor as they emerged into the tall-ceilinged chamber into which the two waterfalls emptied. The rough rock walls were covered with climbing goblins, the floor littered with a dozen more that seemed too tired or injured—or just plain scared—to start the climb back up to Cavemouth territory.

It was Glnk who started shouting at them first, then Lidda piped in. The goblins didn't stop all at once. It took painfully long minutes of grunting back and forth, the harsh sounds echoing from the walls and often ending up lost under the hissing of the waterfalls, before they started to climb back down.

Jozan wanted to pray again but already felt as if he was pressing his luck.

Regdar kept an eye on Tzrg but tried hard to keep the contempt he felt for the goblin from coming through in his expression.

Tzrg was the chief of the Stonedeep Tribe. He should have been looking out for his people, but instead, he'd let Rezrex take over, destroy what seemed to have been a reasonable peace with the Cavemouth Tribe, and spread havoc not only through their own cold, damp, dark caves but up onto the surface world as well.

A lot of blood had been spilled because Tzrg was a weak leader.

The goblin regarded Regdar with a mixture of fear and hope—mostly fear. It was plain to the human that the goblin chief was as intimidated by him as he was by Rezrex. The fact that Tzrg's loyalty to Rezrex had crumbled the second he was separated from the hobgoblin was something Regdar wouldn't soon forget. Would Tzrg be as loyal to Regdar when he next encountered Rezrex?

It was a question Regdar itched to have answered. Standing back at the mouth of the side-passage while Lidda, Jozan, and the other goblin chief went off with the queen spider to rally the fleeing Cavemouth goblins, Regdar was anxious to get on with it. Naull was still out there somewhere, and it seemed as if every second that passed was a second she might not be able to spare, or a second she might not want to have to live through.

As the damnable magic light finally faded from Rezrex's eyes, he growled in pain and anger but knew he would have his revenge.

This man named Regdar was strong—strong enough to kill both of his beloved and valuable krenshars—but he would pay for that particular insult with his blood and his female's.

"Gorvon," he called, blinking the purple splotches from his vision.

The hobgoblin he'd known all his life—his cousin, actually—and one of only two of his own kind left for him to command, stood awaiting instructions, himself blinking away the aftereffects of the human female's magic light.

"Gorvon," Rezrex grumbled, "tell me you brought some of those damn goblins with you."

Gorvon nodded and gestured behind him. Rezrex's darkvision cleared enough for him to see the silhouettes of more than a dozen goblins, shuffling nervously behind Gorvon. They brought some of their hive spiders with them, too, and Rezrex forced a smile.

"Good," he said, clapping a hand firmly on Gorvon's broad shoulder. "The rest of the little shite-eaters who ran will be punished later, eh?"

Gorvon smiled himself, revealing broken yellow teeth under

his red nose. Gorvon wasn't the smartest of Rezrex's tight little gang, but he was a good fighter—good with a spiked chain—and he could take a hit when he needed to.

The other hobgoblin, Kadvor, was holding the human female. The sight of her made Rezrex's smile fade into a grimace. She wasn't much to look at: skinny, soft, and she smelled strange. Blood was trickling down her chin from her nose, which still looked too small and too pointy. He could see that Kadvor was getting curious, and Rezrex thought maybe the human female smelled different close up. After he had a chance to use her against Regdar, he didn't care what Kadvor did with her.

"Put your dagger to her throat, Kadvor," Rezrex commanded. "I want the man to worry—and he will, if what I hear about human mating rites is true."

Kadvor smirked and drew his heavy, serrated dagger.

"When I give the word," Rezrex continued, "slice her to the spine, but—" he held up a finger— "not before I say so."

Kadvor's smirk twisted into a disappointed grimace, but he nodded.

Turning, Rezrex faced the assembled goblins and counted fifteen of them. They'd brought six of the spiders. He didn't doubt the human could kill them all, but with the female up his sleeve, Rezrex didn't think it would come to that.

He slid his mace from behind his back and held it high. The goblins were afraid of him enough to quiet down and stop jittering when they saw it. The weapon was impressive, even to Rezrex. It was given to him by his father—or, more to the point, he'd taken it from his father's dead hand—who had stolen it from a human priest who was guarding a caravan his father had robbed. It was a fine weapon that everyone around him assumed was enchanted, and maybe it was. Rezrex did fight better with it than any weapon he'd ever used.

"The man," he shouted to the assembled goblins, "has dared to desecrate the caves of the Stonedeep Tribe! Find him, and the enemy chief Glnk, and k—"

The goblins stared at him blankly, and Rezrex huffed, realizing he'd been speaking his native tongue. When he talked to goblins, he had to talk like he was addressing an infant.

"*Vrmvs bkn!*" he shouted—Find man. "*Vrmvs Glnk! Bwlnk bkn!*"—Kill man—"*Bwlnk Glnk! Dfln Rezrex!*"—Stonedeep belongs to Rezrex—"*Klsn Rezrex!*"—Cavemouth belongs to Rezrex—"*Gbn Rezrex!*"—Goblins belong to Rezrex.

The goblins started bouncing up and down on their toes, gathering their courage, and Rezrex knew they'd do what he told them to do. He wanted them to follow him, he wanted them to attack.

He screamed the battle cry: "*Gnrbt gbn! Pnlrd gbn!*"

Follow me, goblins! Attack, goblins!

The pain in Regdar's right leg had dwindled to a dull throb that was easy enough for him to ignore. He was running, which was loosening the muscles, and he was finally on the way to confront Rezrex and rescue Naull, and that made him feel better too. His blood was racing through his veins, his senses were growing more acute, his muscles were tensing for the fight to come. Even running down the uneven rocky cave floor through darkness cut through only by bobbing wedges of torchlight, Regdar was in his element.

Behind him were Jozan—clanking along in his unsubtle armor—Lidda, her lanternlight strangely absent, the two goblin chiefs, and maybe a score or more of the Cavemouth goblins. The hive spider queen took up the rear, emitting an irregular series of clicks and whistles as it scurried along. The sounds popped and pinged off the walls and stalactites, mixing with the footsteps and grunts of the goblins, and the clattering of spider feet that seemed to come from everywhere at once.

Regdar didn't let his attention wander to the spiders, but he could sense them gathering. They came from every crack, behind every stalagmite and stalactite. They were on the ceiling above and behind him, and on the walls all around. They were coming from everywhere, answering the calls of their queen.

Several of the Cavemouth goblins were carrying torches behind him, and at the edge of their wavering light Regdar could make out the shape of the hulking hobgoblin. Though he couldn't see well enough to be sure, Regdar got the sense that there were others behind it. He couldn't see Naull.

Regdar, his greatsword trailing behind him in his right hand, ready for a running slash, his shield in front of him to deflect javelins or whatever might be thrown or fired at him, ran into the fight, anxious to get on with it.

Jozan's voice rose above the din of the massed charge, and Regdar smiled when he heard the prayer to Pelor, the Shining One, God of the Sun, ring through the cave. He could feel the power of the prayer wash over him—they were no mere words. It was as if the sun somehow broke through the two thousand feet or more of rock above them to shine on Regdar and the cause for which he fought. Pelor himself would help guide his hand—for the sake of justice.

By the time Regdar—and, more importantly, the torchlight behind him—was close enough to see that the hobgoblin in front wasn't Rezrex, it was too late for the human to turn his charge. The hobgoblin—obviously one of Rezrex's cronies—was spinning a heavy length of chain studded with cruel, curved spikes. The polished steel links reflected flashes of orange from the bobbing torchlight and made the first attack harder to see.

Regdar brought his shield up just in time to block the chain that was speeding toward his face. The cruel weapon clanged off the protective metal, and Regdar batted it away. The hobgoblin drew the weapon back in with a flick of his wrist in the time it took for Regdar to get within slashing range.

The chain whipped up and past the hobgoblin's right side and in front of him to wrap around Regdar's blade. The hobgoblin made the mistake of trying to pull Regdar's greatsword toward him, hoping to yank it from the human's grip. Regdar, whose hand was wrapped around the comfortable pommel of the greatsword like an iron vise, leaped into the air. The combination of the momentum of his charge, the leap itself, and the hobgoblin yanking on the chain wrapped around his sword pulled Regdar through the air and onto the hobgoblin so fast and so hard it sent both of them sprawling.

Regdar didn't know the hobgoblin was standing in front of a pool of ice-cold water until they both splashed into it, arms and legs splaying, bodies twisting in the air in mixed attempts to land on their feet, avoid each others' weapons, or kill each other. Before he had a chance to worry that he'd sink again, he hit the bottom of the shallow pool hard enough to drive a grunt from his chest and make his ears ring.

He felt the hobgoblin under him and jammed his knee down, pushing himself up. When the hobgoblin rolled out from beneath him, Regdar almost went back under but managed to scramble away, his back scraping against a rock wall that rose out of the middle of the shallow pool like a column that disappeared into the darkness over his head.

He drew in a deep breath the second his head came out of the water, and he blinked to clear his eyes. The hobgoblin was in front of him, just at the edge of the pool and was sputtering and coughing up water even as it gathered its spiked chain in a coil. Behind the hobgoblin, Glnk was smashing apart the dull brown carapace of a hive spider.

Regdar took one step forward in the water, which slowed him considerably. His greatsword was raised above his head, ready for a downward hack at the hobgoblin, when a roaring voice shattered his concentration.

"Stop!" Rezrex shouted, stepping into the torchlight, a third hobgoblin at his side.

Jozan shouted, "Naull!"

The hobgoblin with Rezrex was holding the young mage with one of his big, brutish arms wrapped around her chest. Blood was seeping from her nose, and a huge bruise was blossoming on her round face. She was hanging limp in the hobgoblin's grip, eyes closed. She was breathing, but Regdar feared she wouldn't be for long. In his other hand, the hobgoblin held a wicked serrated dagger, similar to the one that had mangled Regdar's leg. He was holding the weapon to Naull's soft, exposed throat.

Rezrex laughed, and Regdar's blood boiled.

"Stop now, man!" Rezrex called. "Stop now or female bleeds out!"

The hobgoblin with the spiked chain stepped up out of the pool, regarding Regdar with cold contempt.

Rezrex grinned and said, "I give word—*one word!*—and female is—"

The hobgoblin was interrupted by a feral shriek from Glnk. The new chief of the Cavemouth Tribe, oblivious to Naull's danger, rushed at the hobgoblin, brandishing a stone club that was still dripping with the hive spider's sticky yellow ichor, and traces of the spidersilk that marked it as one of the bars from the queen spider's cage.

Regdar wanted to scream for the goblin to stop, but the chief wouldn't have understood him, as he hadn't understood Rezrex, who was speaking his grunting, halting Common.

Like it was all happening underwater, muddy and slow, Regdar watched the goblin charge, saw Rezrex open his mouth to give the order to cut Naull's throat—

—and the word "*Silence!*" boomed through the cave.

It was Jozan, using the grace of Pelor the same way he'd made Lidda scream to reveal herself in the woods on the surface. The hobgoblin's throat visibly tensed, and the word or grunt or command that was about to be issued stopped there as if it had substance and weight.

Regdar looked back at Naull, still hanging limply in the arms of the hobgoblin. The humanoid was looking at his chief, awaiting the order to kill the helpless woman as if it was something he was dying to do. When his eyes went wide, Regdar took a splashing step forward and opened his mouth to scream. It looked like the hobgoblin was going to kill her anyway, maybe sensing Rezrex's interrupted intention.

When the hobgoblin dropped the dagger, Regdar actually gasped. There was blood, and he thought it was Naull's but realized soon enough that it was the hobgoblin who was bleeding.

A face passed into the light from behind the falling hobgoblin—a long, oval face as small as a little girl's, but with an executioner's grim countenance. It was Lidda—she'd sneaked up behind the hobgoblin and stabbed it with her short sword before it could kill Naull. Regdar wanted to kiss the halfling thief, wanted to buy her a drink, wanted to do whatever she wanted him to do.

A strangled, incoherent growl rose in volume and intensity, tearing its way out of Rezrex's throat, and Regdar knew the spell was spent. The hobgoblin who had been holding Naull dropped her and turned on Lidda. It was still alive.

The halfling backed into the darkness, then Regdar's attention was drawn to the spiked chain that wrapped around his shield, slapping hard into his vambrace to bruise his left forearm.

He pulled back on his shield, which bent a little at the edges under the chain, and the hobgoblin flicked its wrist again. The chain unwound fast, and though Regdar bent his neck painfully to avoid it, one of the spikes traced a line across his left cheek, drawing blood but missing his eye.

Glnk, still charging, crashed into Rezrex, and the hobgoblin chief roared with rage. The goblin got a good hit into the hobgoblin's midsection with his stone club, but Rezrex stepped back and pushed Glnk to the side with his left hand while his right hand brought the beautifully crafted mace down hard at Glnk's head.

Behind Rezrex were a group of goblins—Stonedeep goblins—who moved up, grunting and brandishing javelins, clubs, and other weapons Regdar couldn't see. The cave was filled with a thousand echoed grunts as Tzrg ran up toward the advancing goblins, grunting at them.

Regdar could only hope that Tzrg was convincing them to abandon Rezrex. If Tzrg didn't take the Stonedeep Tribe back from the hobgoblin usurper, the enraged, fatherless Glnk would kill them all if it took the rest of his life—Rezrex or no Rezrex.

Regdar, splashing through the cold water, advanced on the hobgoblin with the spiked chain, knowing he had to get in close or eventually the humanoid would manage to get the thing wrapped around his arm, his neck, his head—and disarm or kill him. He ducked low under a swing from the chain and tried to bat it with his shield when it came around again. He missed, and the hobgoblin twisted the chain, so it whipped up over Regdar's head, only to come in lower the next pass. Regdar, knowing that's what he would have done himself, was ready for that, though, and he got his shield low and batted the chain out and away, breaking its momentum enough to send it splashing into the water.

If it wasn't covered with sharp spikes, Regdar would have stepped on the chain as the hobgoblin drew it back in. Instead, he made use of the time to advance closer into the hobgoblin while glancing over at Naull, who was lying still but breathing on the rock floor near the edge of the pool. The bleeding hobgoblin had dropped its dagger when Lidda cut its arm, but it had drawn a shining, sweeping-bladed falchion. The hobgoblin looked strong, but it was dumb and slow. Lidda seemed to be avoiding its one inept hack after the other, but she was slowly being backed up against the wall, and Regdar knew that her short sword wouldn't stand up to the hobgoblin's much heavier blade.

Tzrg was still grunting at his goblins, and Regdar could see the little humanoids' eyes following the spiders that were all the while gathering around the released queen. This seemed to impress them, and they stopped their advance.

Glnk was having a difficult time holding Rezrex off, but Regdar could see Jozan advancing to help him.

Regdar heard the chain whipping through the air and realized that he had to kill this hobgoblin before he could help either Jozan or Lidda—and both of them needed his help and needed it badly.

He didn't realize he'd closed his eyes when he hacked down at the hobgoblin, but he had. It wasn't so much finesse and skill now as it was just brute force—the single-minded will to cleave his opponent.

The greatsword shuddered as it passed through skin, bone, lung, heart, bone, liver, bone, skin, and back out, leaving a twitching, bloody mess to splash dead into the cold water.

When he opened his eyes, Regdar saw that Glnk had tripped or been forced down in front of the raging Rezrex. The huge mace was coming down fast, and Regdar knew there was no way he could get there in time to stop Glnk from being killed.

A flash of yellow and brown appeared in front of him and in the time it took for Regdar to take a single water-slowed step, Tzrg smashed into Glnk, pushing the Cavemouth chief out of the way of the mace. When the weapon came down, it smashed into Tzrg's calf. Regdar heard the loud snap of Tzrg's leg breaking, then heard it over and over again as it echoed through the cave.

The Stonedeep goblins gasped as one, and Tzrg opened his mouth to scream, but no sound came out. The goblin turned an even sicklier shade of yellow, and his eyes rolled into his skull.

"Regdar!" Lidda called. "Jozan! A little help here!"

Regdar saw that she'd been backed into the wall, and he shifted his momentum to try to get to her. The water was slowing him down when he needed most to move quickly.

Glnk, still rolling from Tzrg's life-saving shove, slid to a halt into the back of the hobgoblin's legs, though, and a swipe of the falchion that might have beheaded Lidda went wide when the humanoid had to hop to keep its feet. Lidda took fast advantage of the opening and jabbed the hobgoblin. The thing was wearing pieces of thick hide interlaced with bone and scraps of metal, so her blade didn't dig as deeply into the thing as Lidda obviously hoped it would, but the hobgoblin howled in pain in any case.

Regdar came out of the pool between the stumbling hobgoblin and Rezrex, just as Rezrex roared at the still helplessly writhing Tzrg and started to bring the enchanted mace down on the goblin's head.

The big hobgoblin was just at the edge of the reach of Regdar's greatsword, but that was enough. Regdar threw himself to the side, knowing he would fall at the hobgoblin's feet, swinging his sword with him.

The blade took Rezrex's right hand off at the wrist, sending it— and the beautiful enchanted mace—whirling into the air trailing blood and slivers of bone.

The roar that burst from the wounded hobgoblin was almost deafening and made Regdar's ears ring only worse. He hit the ground so hard his own spiked rander sent his pauldron into his shoulder hard enough to break the skin.

The Stonedeep goblins, apparently finally inspired, stopped their senseless face down of the Cavemouth goblins and poured like a yellow-skinned tide around the hobgoblin who was trying to kill Lidda.

The hobgoblin whirled on the goblins, brandishing the falchion, and Regdar saw Lidda slip back into the deep black shadows. The goblins fell on the already wounded hobgoblin, and it went down in a mass of javelins, kicks, stone clubs, and tiny little fists.

Regdar rolled away from Rezrex and almost tripped Jozan. On the way, Regdar saw Glnk toss the serrated dagger that had been being held to Naull's throat. Tzrg caught it, his face still twisted with agony. Before Rezrex could gather his own wits, Tzrg drove the heavy blade into the hobgoblin's gut. The look of surprise on Rezrex's face was almost comical.

Glnk jumped to his feet, and when Tzrg's hand slipped off the dagger handle, leaving it protruding from the hobgoblin's ample gut, Glnk took hold of it. There was an unpleasant ripping sound as Glnk dragged the blade up and in a long, curving arc, leaving a line of red that exploded outward, spilling Rezrex's steaming guts to the cave floor.

Epilogue... Spending a night with a tribe of goblins was about the last thing Regdar thought he'd ever do, but after the day he'd had, a little quiet and a chance to close his eyes made the Stonedeep caves seem like the most luxurious inn in New Koratia.

Naull wasn't badly hurt, and once they got her some water and Lidda carefully cleaned the blood from her face, she hardly looked the worse for wear. In the dim torchlight, deep in the savage caves, it was hard to see the bruise.

"I feel like I let you down yesterday," she said, as a groveling female goblin slid a plate of fried cave beetles in front of her. Naull suppressed a gag and pushed the plate away. "All that, and I was lying there unconscious."

Regdar smiled, trying to ignore Jozan who was poking at the wounds on his leg.

"You let no one down," the fighter said, "and you'll never have to prove your courage to me again. You followed me down that tunnel, into the thick of the goblins. Your spells have saved all our lives, and your mind . . . Well, I might be able to swing a sword better than you, but you're smarter than me."

The young woman smiled and looked down. Regdar didn't want to invade her privacy by looking to see if she was blushing. He knew she was.

"Yeah," Lidda said, swaggering up behind them holding a plate of fried beetles, "get a room you two." She popped one of the horrid bugs into her mouth and crunched it, smiling. "These aren't bad."

Jozan began a prayer to Pelor, and Regdar closed his eyes, shuddering under the warmth of the healing spell.

"That looks good," the priest said. "By Pelor's grace, you should only need a second, and we'll be ready to start the climb out of here. It should be almost midday above."

The priest looked up into the darkness, the ceiling invisible in the gloom.

Tzrg was limping, his leg healed by Jozan, much to the amazement of the assembled goblins. It would be several weeks before the little humanoid would be fully healed, but the pain was gone, and Tzrg's gratitude was obvious in the goblin's simple expressions. Glnk was with him, and he was cradling Rezrex's magnificent mace in his hands. The chief of the Cavemouth tribe held the weapon out to Jozan, and Tzrg grumbled some words to Lidda.

"They want you to have the mace," Lidda translated around another fried beetle.

Jozan reached up and took the weapon in one hand.

Glnk smiled and said something to Lidda.

"He's going home," she said. "He'll take us with him, to the bottom of the shaft."

"Ready for a climb?" Naull asked.

Regdar looked at her, and she winked at him.

"We left our horses in Fairbye," Jozan said, still admiring the enchanted mace.

"Lidda," Regdar said, "Naull . . . is Fairbye on your way to wherever you're going?"

"They won't hang you now," Jozan said to the halfling. "Not without hanging me first."

Lidda sighed and pretended to wipe a tear from her cheek. "Friends?" she squeaked.

"Friends," her three friends replied.

Sembia

The perfect entry point into
the richly detailed world of the
FORGOTTEN REALMS®, this
ground-breaking series continues
with these all-new novels.

HEIRS OF PROPHECY
By Lisa Smedman

The maid Larajin has more secrets in her life than she ever
bargained for, but when an unknown evil fuels a war between
Sembia and the elves of the Tangled Trees, secrets pile on secrets
and threaten to bury her once and for all.

June 2002

SANDS OF THE SOUL
By Voronica Whitney-Robinson

Tazi has never felt so alone. Unable to trust anyone, frightened
of her enemy's malign power, and knowing that it was more
luck than skill that saved her the last time, she comes to realize
that the consequences of the necromancer's plans could shake
the foundations of her world.

November 2002

Revisit Krynn with these great collections!

An all-new anthology of classic
DRAGONLANCE® stories

The Best of Tales, Volume II

Edited by Margaret Weis & Tracy Hickman

This new collection contains a selection of classic DRAGONLANCE
tales and an all-new roleplaying adventure by Tracy Hickman.
This "best of" includes favorites by well-known DRAGONLANCE
authors Douglas Niles, Richard A. Knaak, Paul B. Thompson &
Tonya C. Cook, Dan Parkinson, Roger Moore, and others.

Available now!

The great modern fantasy epic —
now available in paperback

The Annotated Chronicles

Margaret Weis & Tracy Hickman

Margaret Weis & Tracy Hickman return to the Chronicles,
adding notes and commentary in this annotated paperback
edition of the three books that began the epic saga.

October 2002

R.A. Salvatore's
War of the Spider Queen

New York Times best-selling author R.A.
Salvatore, creator of the legendary dark elf
Drizzt Do'Urden, lends his creative genius to
a new FORGOTTEN REALMS® series that delves
deep into the mythic Underdark and even
deeper into the black hearts of the drow.

DISSOLUTION
Book I
Richard Lee Byers sets the stage as the delicate power structure
of Menzoberranzan tilts and threatens to smash apart. When
drow faces drow, only the strongest and most evil can survive.

July 2002

INSURRECTION
Book II
Thomas M. Reid turns up the heat on the drow civil war and
sends the Underdark reeling into chaos. When a god goes silent,
what could possibly set things right?

December 2002

Shandril's Saga

*Ed Greenwood's legendary tales of Shandril
of Highmoon are brought together in this trilogy
that features an all-new finale!*

SPELLFIRE
Book I

"Director's cut" version in an all-new trade paperback edition!

The secret of Spellfire has fallen into the hands of Shandril of
Highmoon. Now the forces of the evil Zhentarim are after her.

April 2002

CROWN OF FIRE
Book II

All-new trade paperback edition!

Shandril and Narm are on the run from the Zhentarim. As
they make their way toward Waterdeep, aided by a motley
band of fighters and mages, the danger grows.

June 2002

New!
HAND OF FIRE
Book III

*Ed Greenwood's latest novel brings
Shandril's Saga to its thrilling conclusion!*

The forces of the Zhentarim and the terrifying Cult of
the Dragon converge on Shandril, but there may be a worse
fate in store for her.

September 2002